Be like Batty—read them all!

Shark and Bot

Sleepaway Champs

Zombie Doughnut Attack!

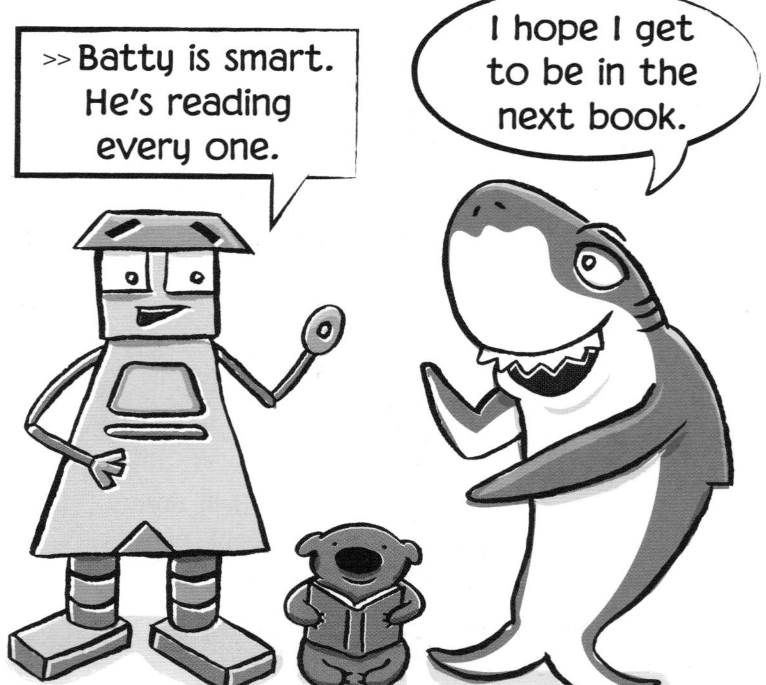
>> Batty is smart. He's reading every one.
I hope I get to be in the next book.

SHARK AND BOT 3

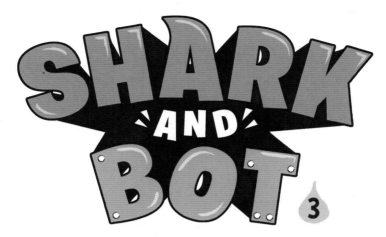

Zombie Doughnut Attack!

>> Are those . . . DOUGHNUTS?

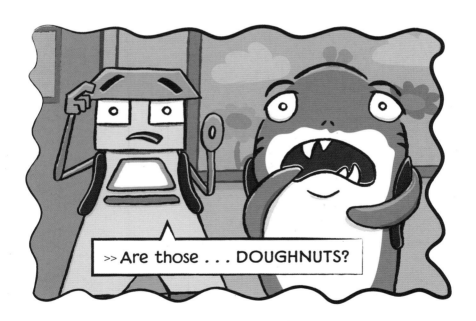

Brian Yanish

A STEPPING STONE BOOK™

Random House New York

All rights reserved. Published in the United States by Random House Children's Books, a division of Penguin Random House LLC, New York.

Random House and the colophon are registered trademarks and A Stepping Stone Book and the colophon are trademarks of Penguin Random House LLC.

RH Graphic with the book design is a trademark of Penguin Random House LLC.

Visit us on the Web! rhcbooks.com

Educators and librarians, for a variety of teaching tools, visit us at RHTeachersLibrarians.com

Library of Congress Cataloging-in-Publication Data is available upon request.
ISBN 978-0-593-48534-7 (hardcover) | ISBN 978-0-593-48536-1 (ebook)

Book design by Jan Gerardi

MANUFACTURED IN CHINA

10 9 8 7 6 5 4 3 2 1

First Edition

For my sister, Lynn

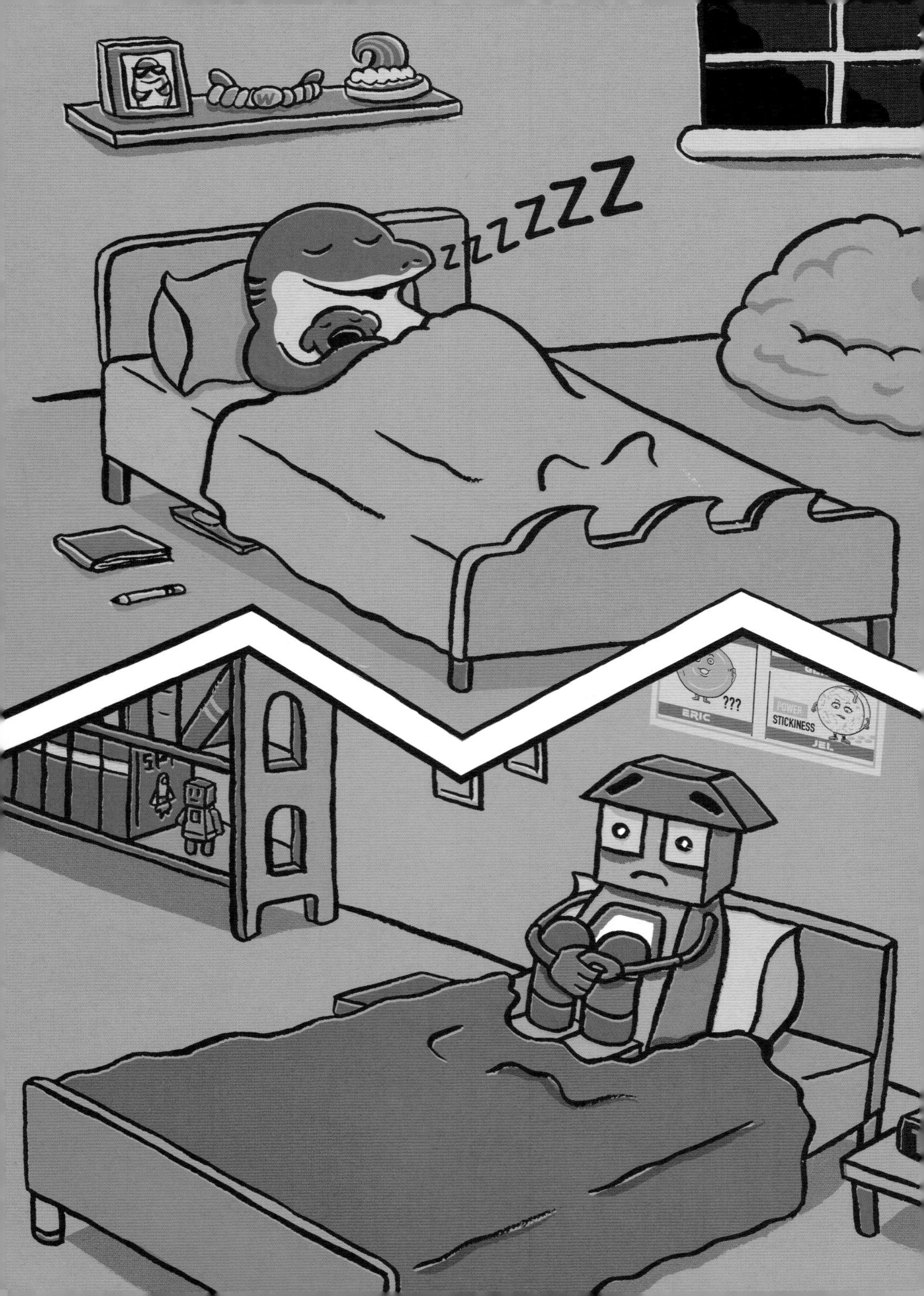
zzzZZZZ
ERIC
???
POWER:
STICKINESS
JEL

Contents

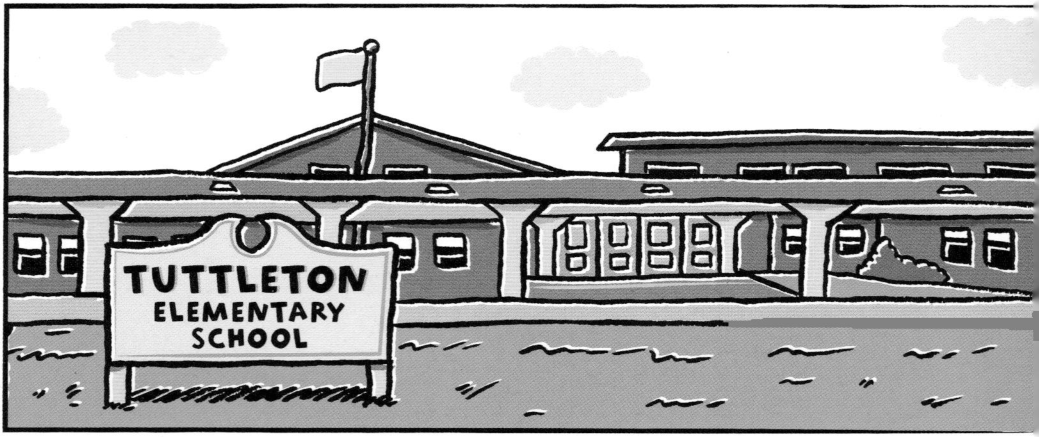
TUTTLETON
ELEMENTARY
SCHOOL

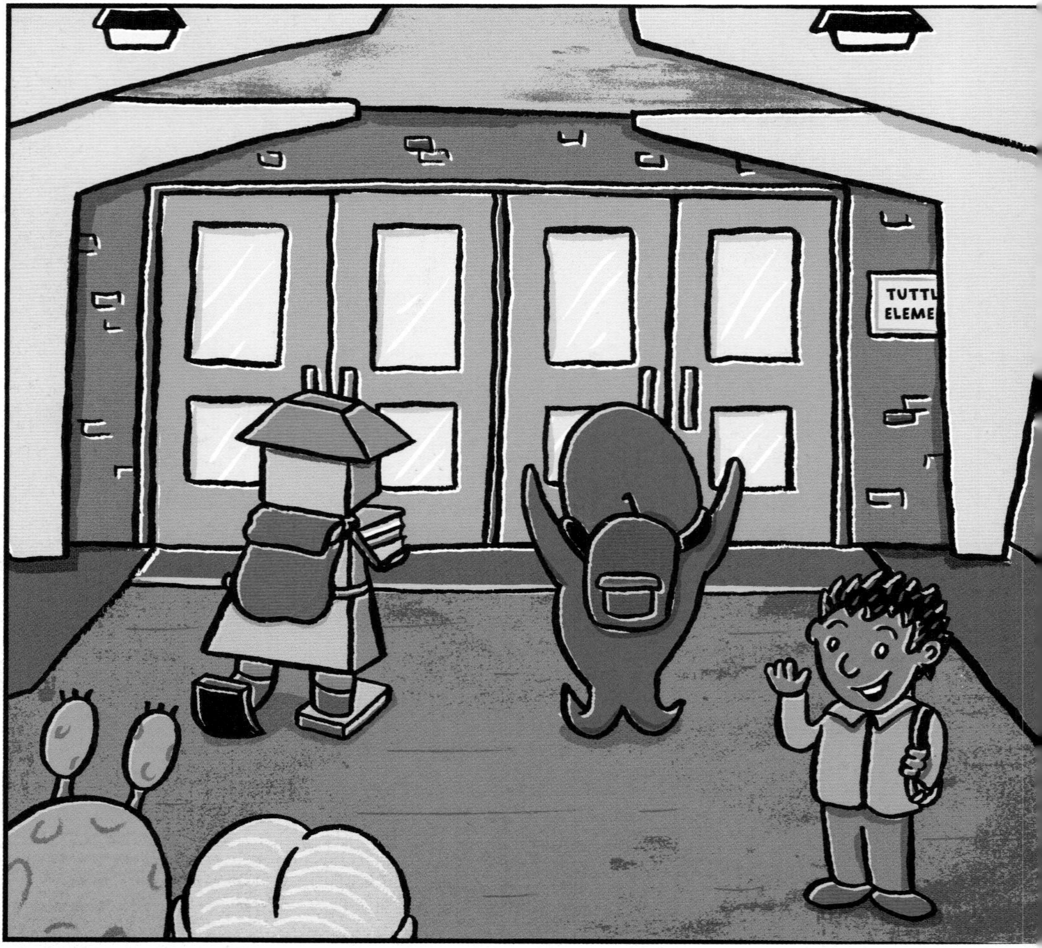

Chapter 1

We Can't Lose

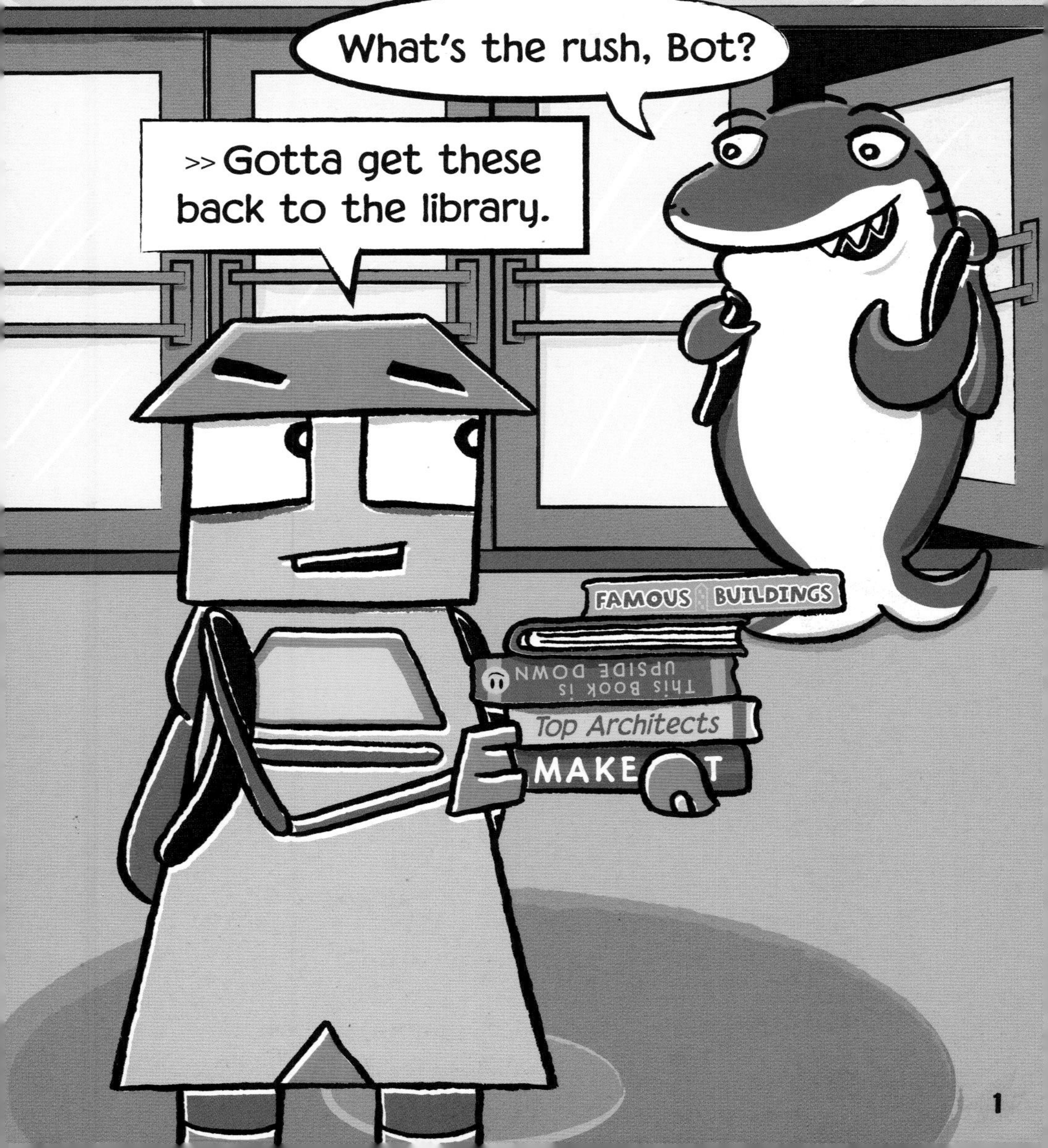

What's the rush, Bot?
>> Gotta get these back to the library.
FAMOUS BUILDINGS
This Book is UPSIDE DOWN
Top Architects
MAKE

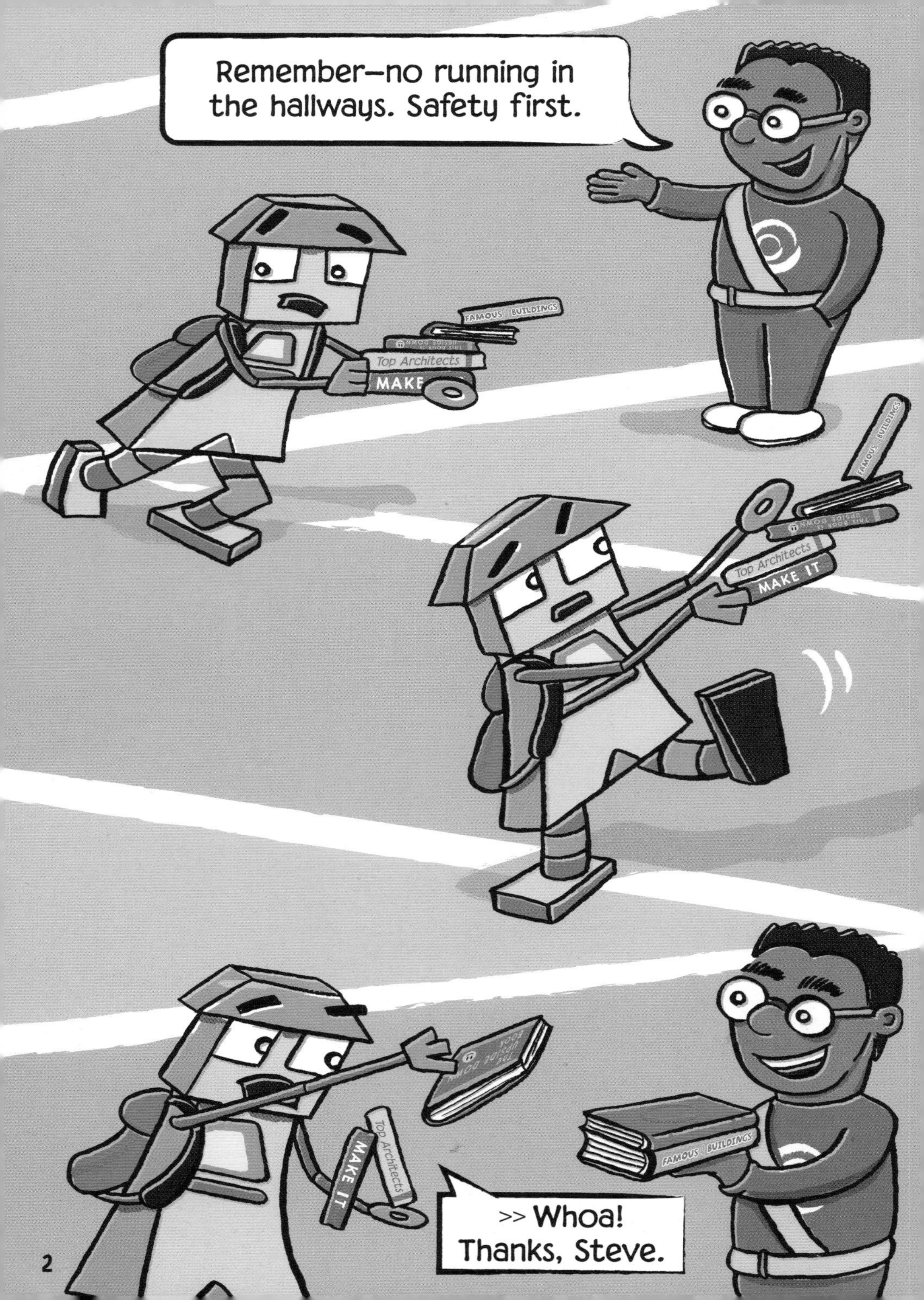
Remember—no running in the hallways. Safety first.
FAMOUS BUILDINGS
Top Architects
MAKE IT
>> Whoa! Thanks, Steve.

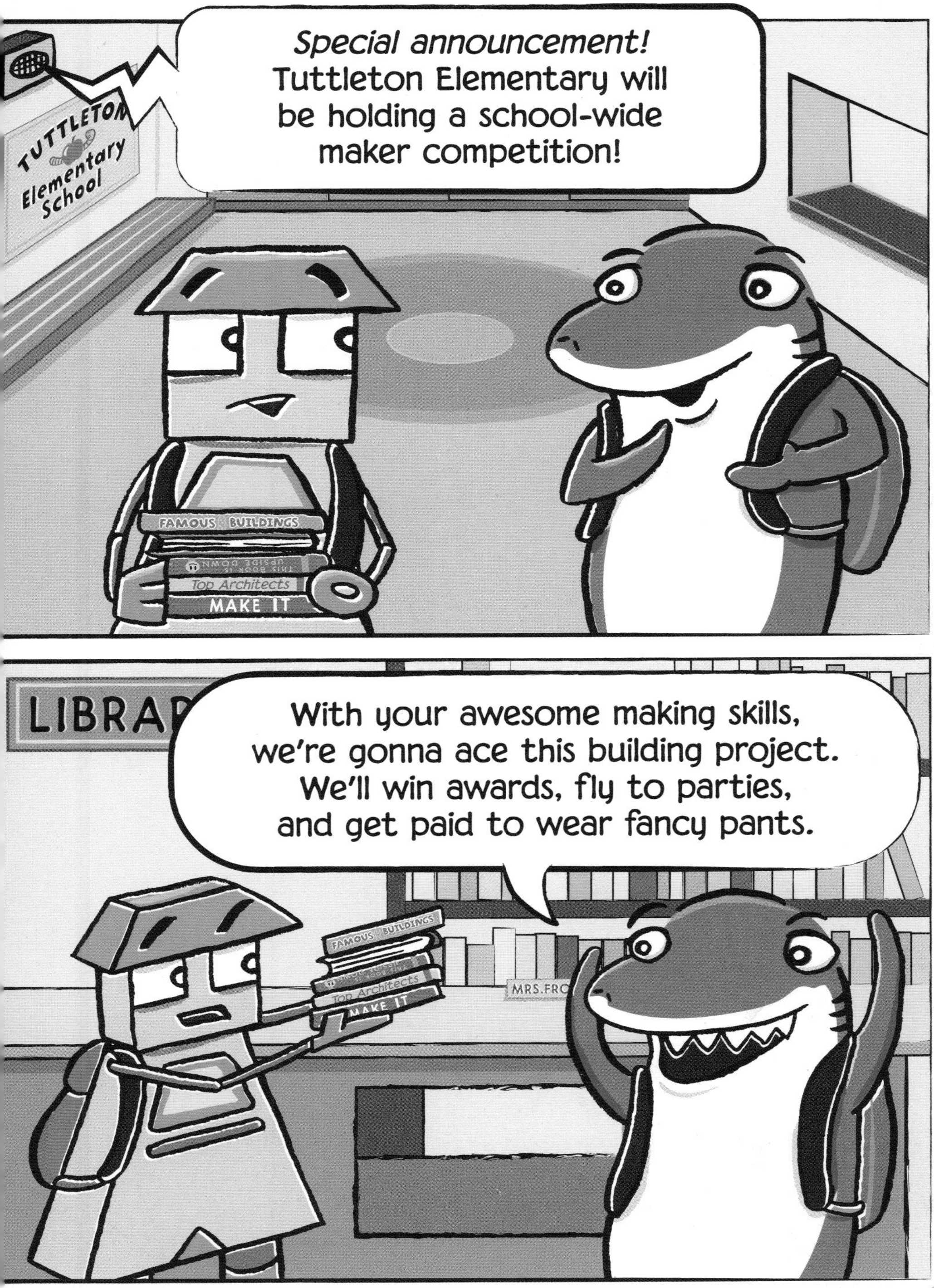
Special announcement! Tuttleton Elementary will be holding a school-wide maker competition!
TUTTLETON Elementary School
FAMOUS BUILDINGS
THIS BOOK IS UPSIDE DOWN
Top Architects
MAKE IT
LIBRAR
With your awesome making skills, we're gonna ace this building project. We'll win awards, fly to parties, and get paid to wear fancy pants.
MRS.FRO

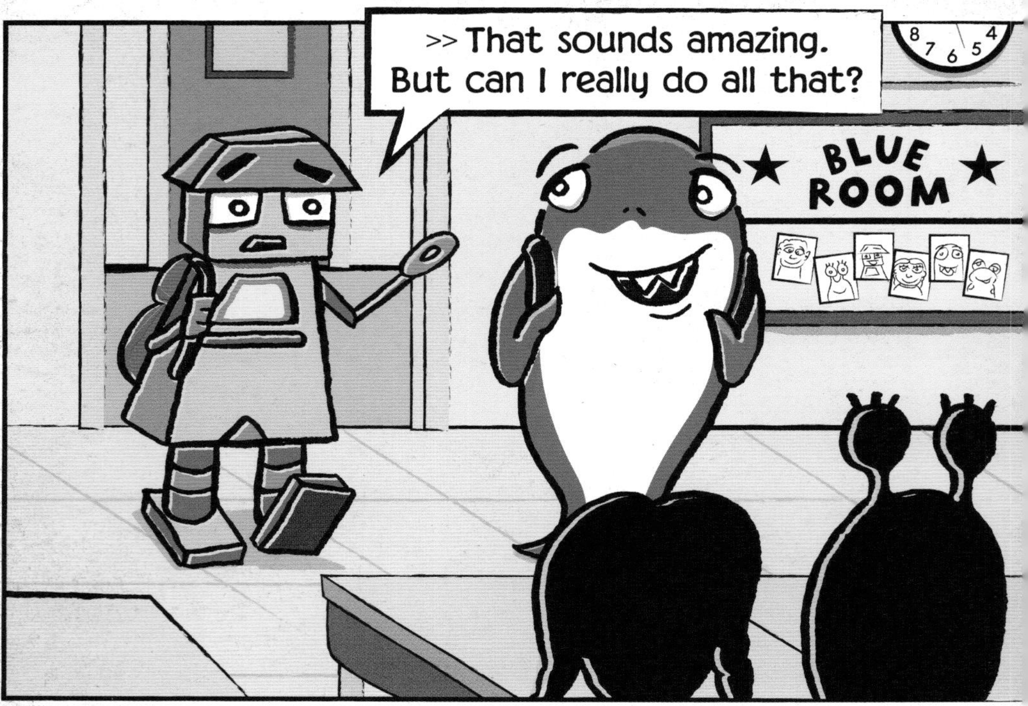
>> That sounds amazing. But can I really do all that?
BLUE ROOM

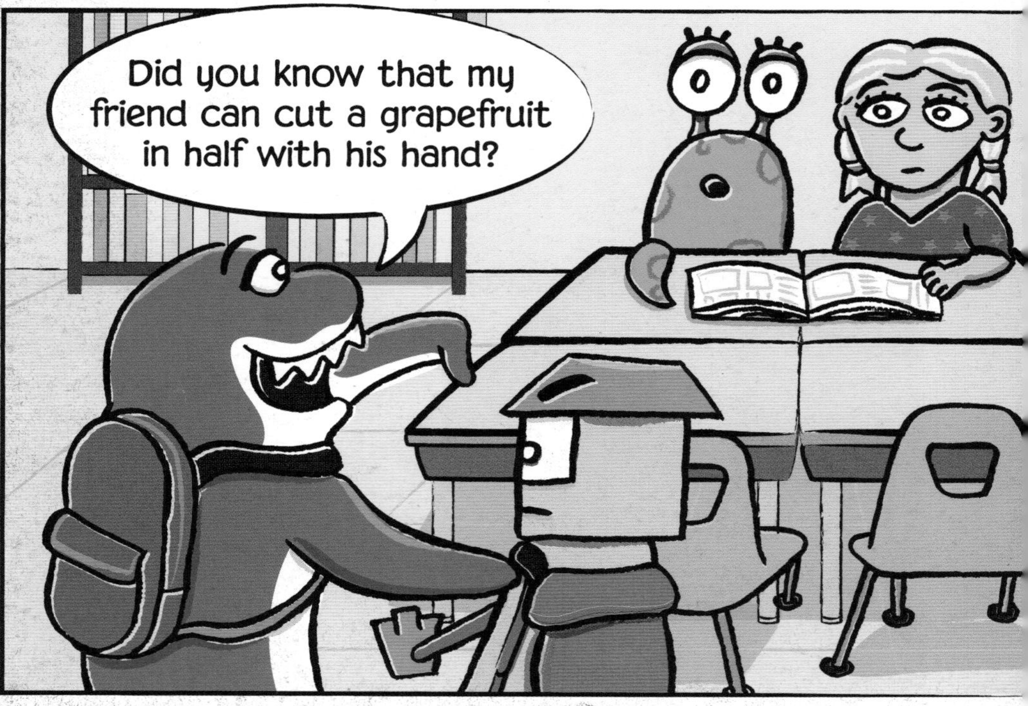
Did you know that my friend can cut a grapefruit in half with his hand?

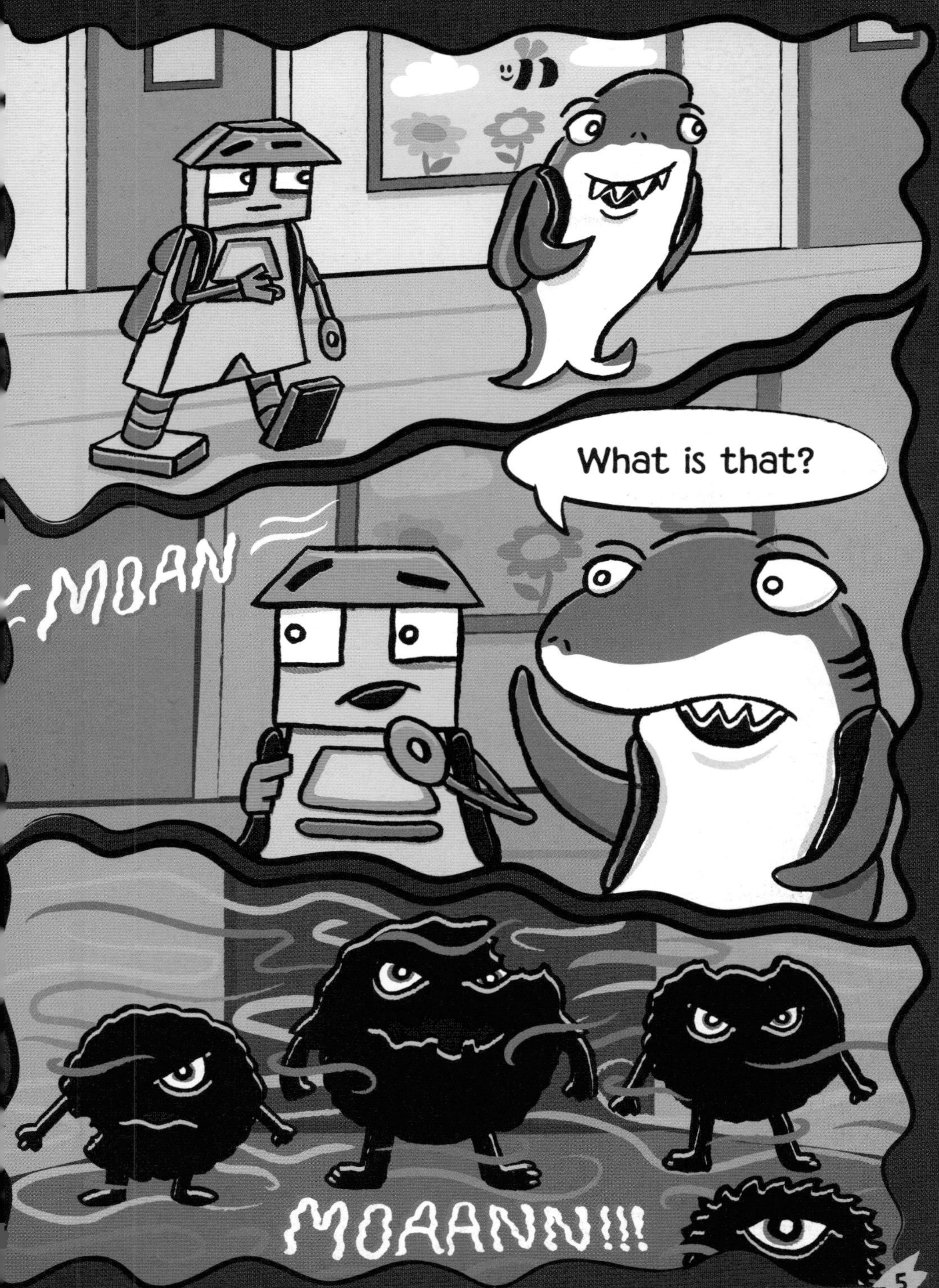
What is that?
MOAN
MOAANN!!!

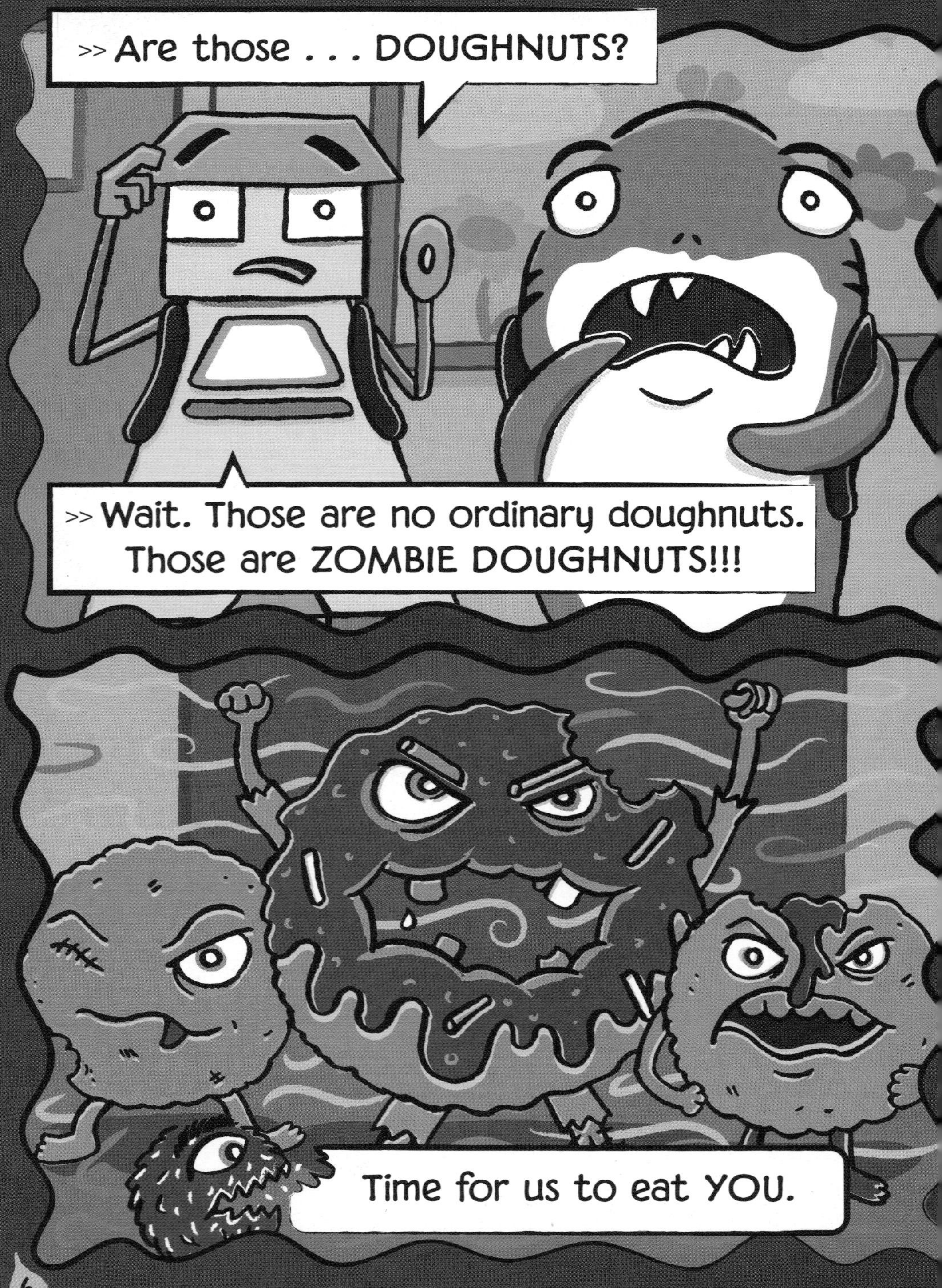
>> Are those . . . DOUGHNUTS?
>> Wait. Those are no ordinary doughnuts. Those are ZOMBIE DOUGHNUTS!!!
Time for us to eat YOU.

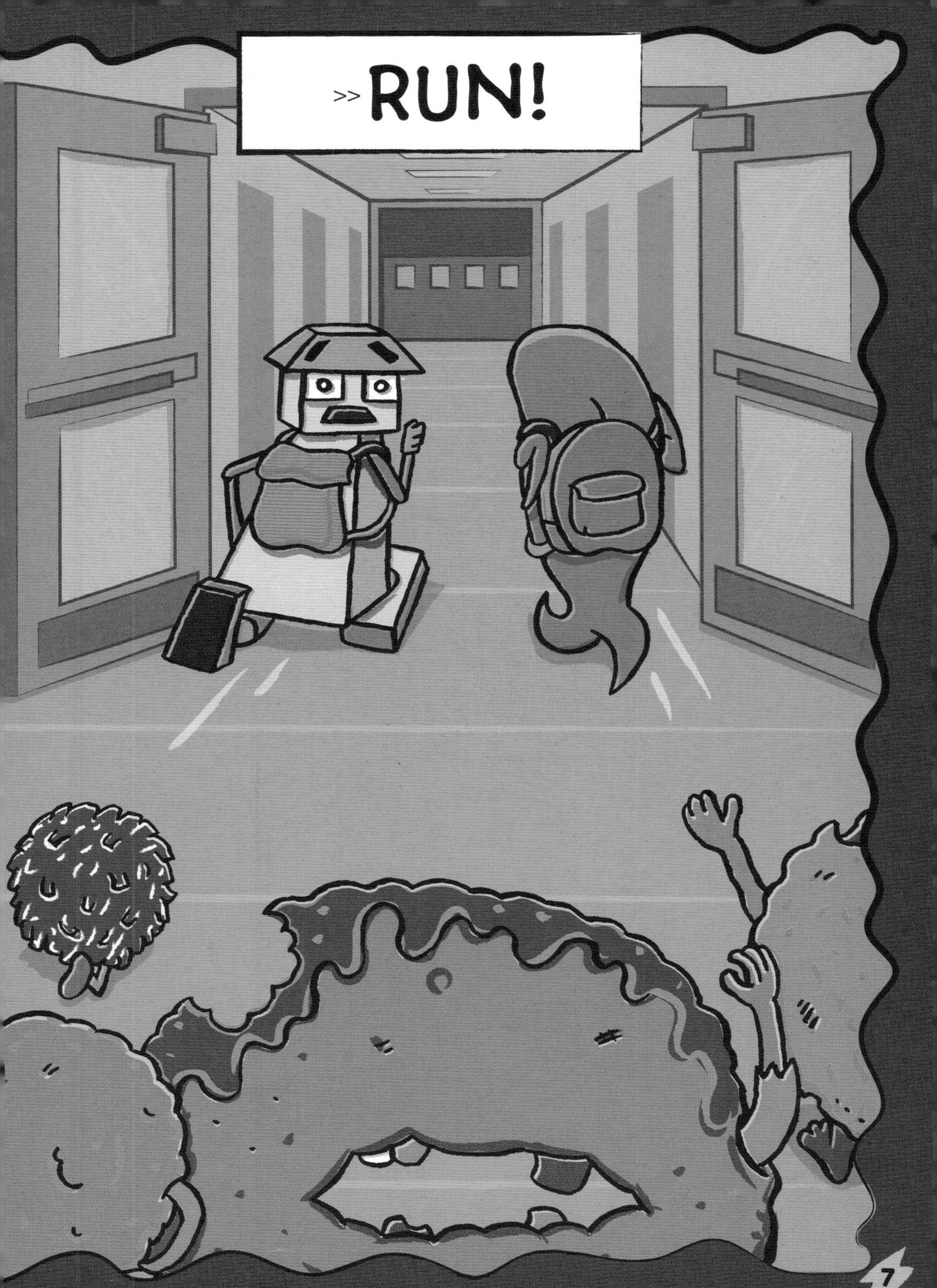
>>RUN!

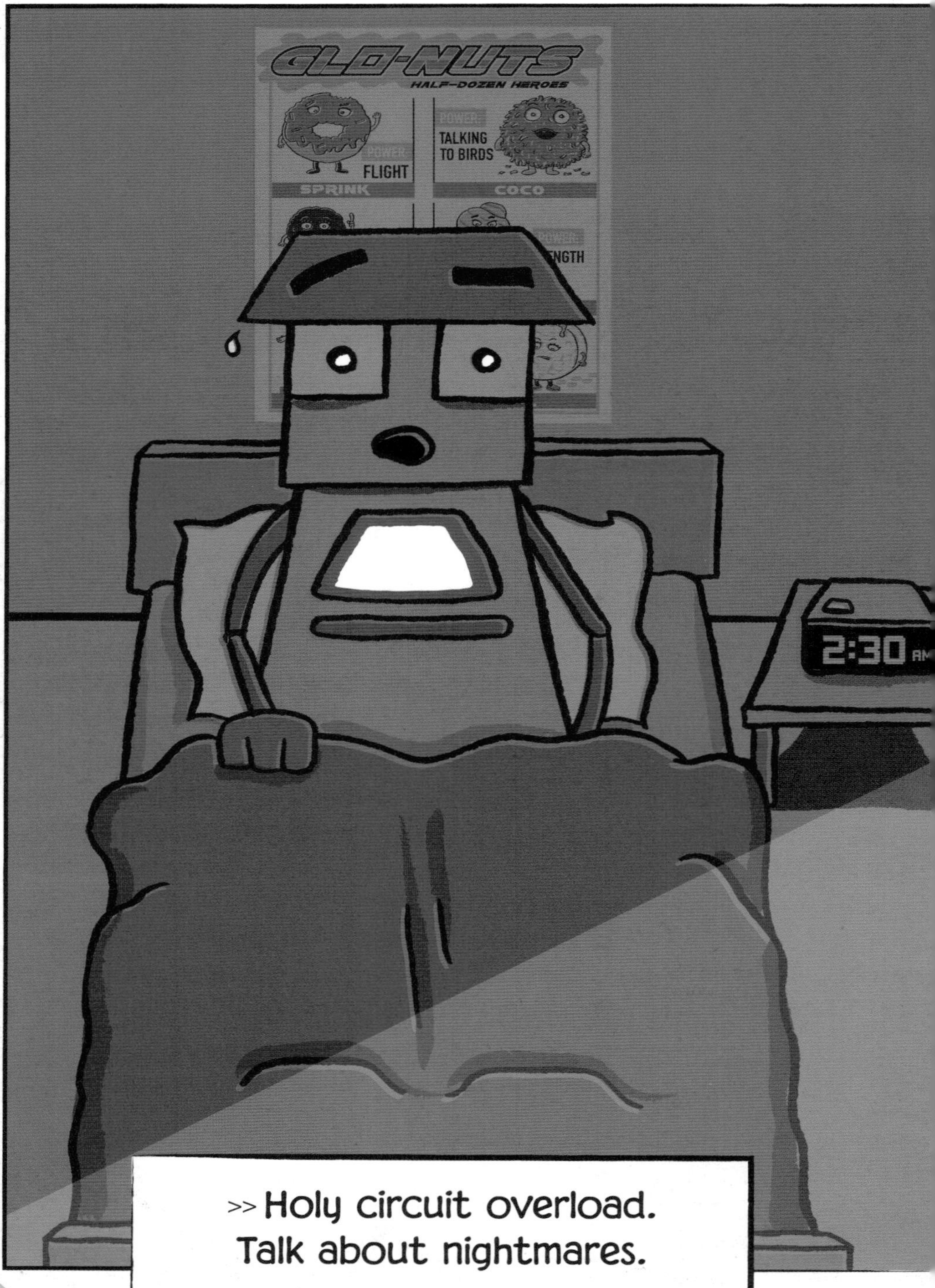
GLO-NUTS
HALF-DOZEN HEROES
POWER: FLIGHT
SPRINK
POWER: TALKING TO BIRDS
COCO
2:30
>> Holy circuit overload.
Talk about nightmares.

Chapter 2

Make It or Break It

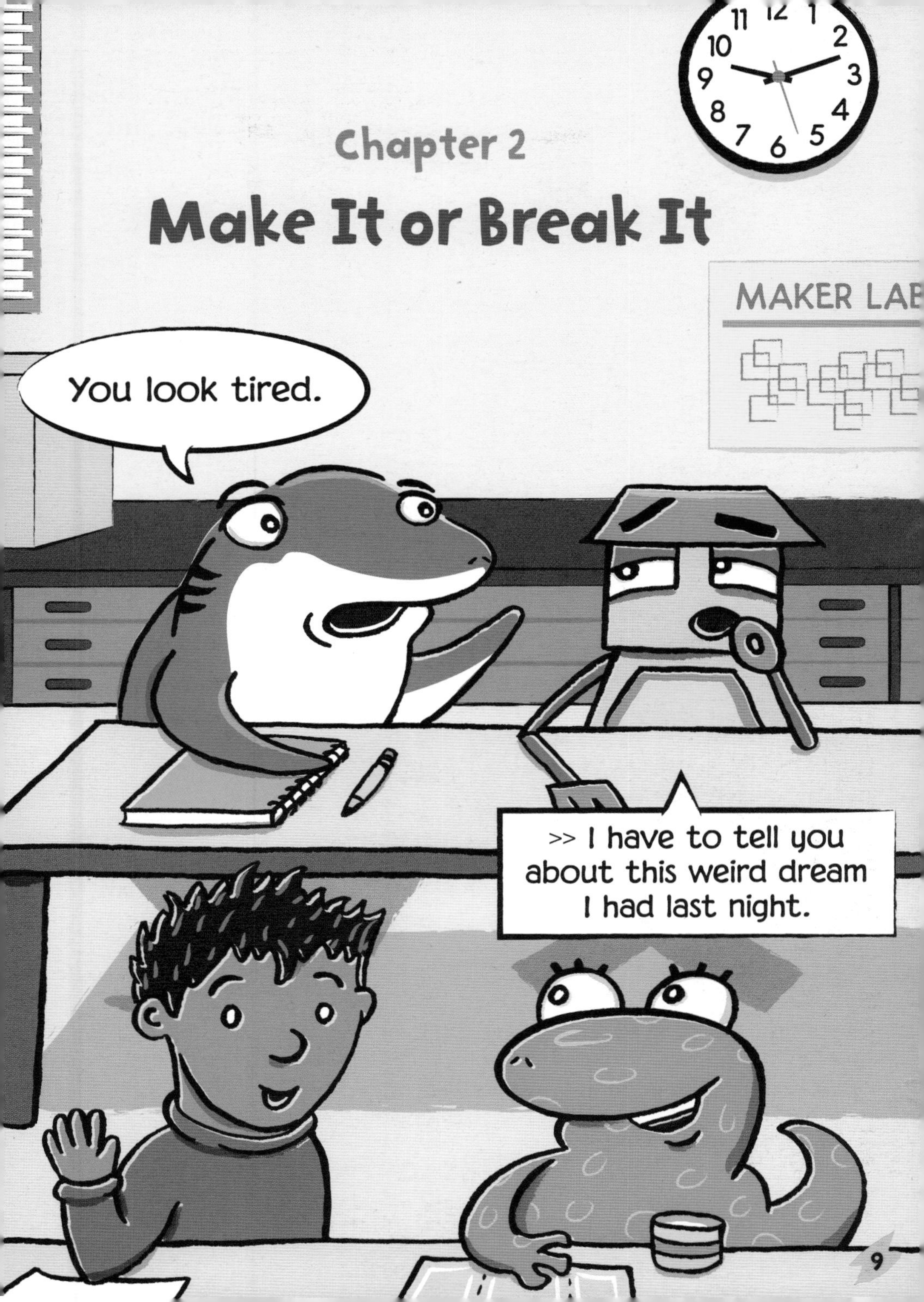
MAKER LAB
You look tired.
>> I have to tell you about this weird dream I had last night.

For Tuttleton's Maker Project, we'll be working in teams to design and construct a model of a building.

SCHOOL MAKER PROJECT

PROJECT: Create a model of a building. It can be anything!

DUE DATE: 1 week from today

WHO: Teams of 2 students

YOUR BUILDING MUST:

1. Have more than 1 room.
2. Have at least one entrance / exit.
3. Be made of some recycled materials.

*You can use the MAKER LAB and ART ROOM supplies, the 3D printer, or any other materials you collect. *You cannot BUY materials.**

YOUR FINAL PROJECT MUST INCLUDE:

1. A map of your building.
2. One written page that describes how your building is used.

QUESTIONS? See Ms. Captain.

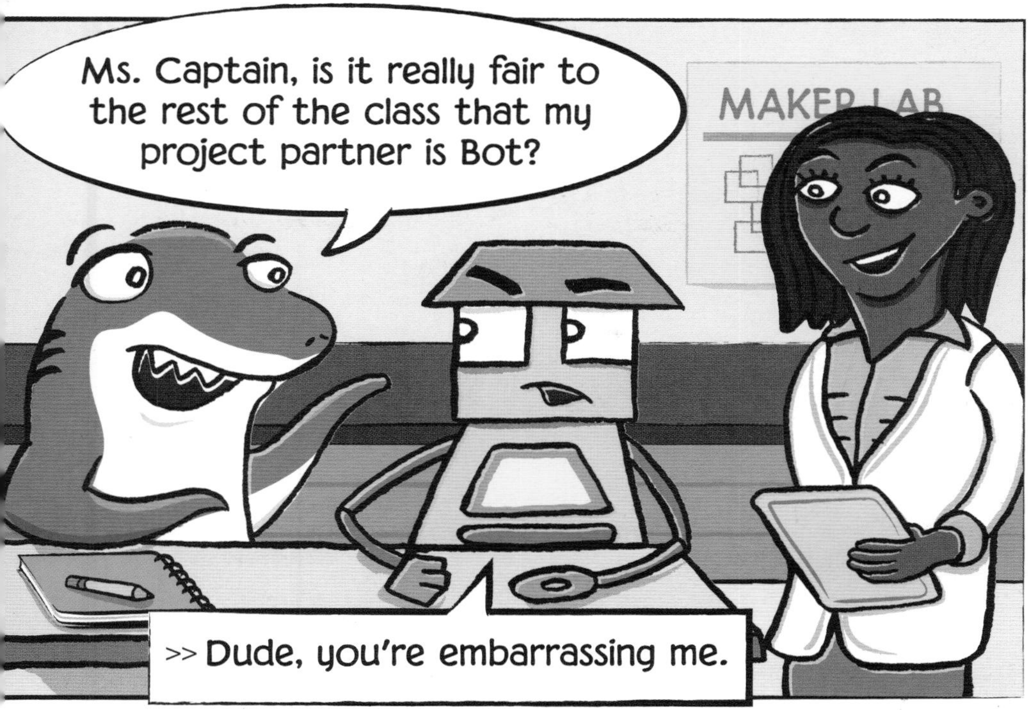
Ms. Captain, is it really fair to the rest of the class that my project partner is Bot?
MAKER LAB
>> Dude, you're embarrassing me.

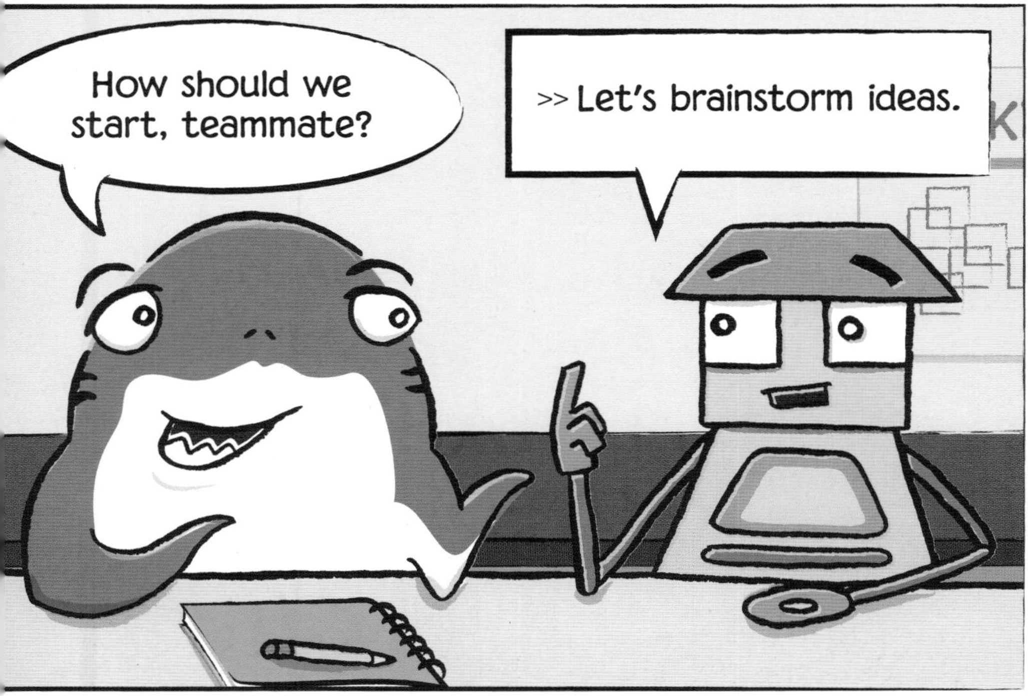
How should we start, teammate?
>> Let's brainstorm ideas.

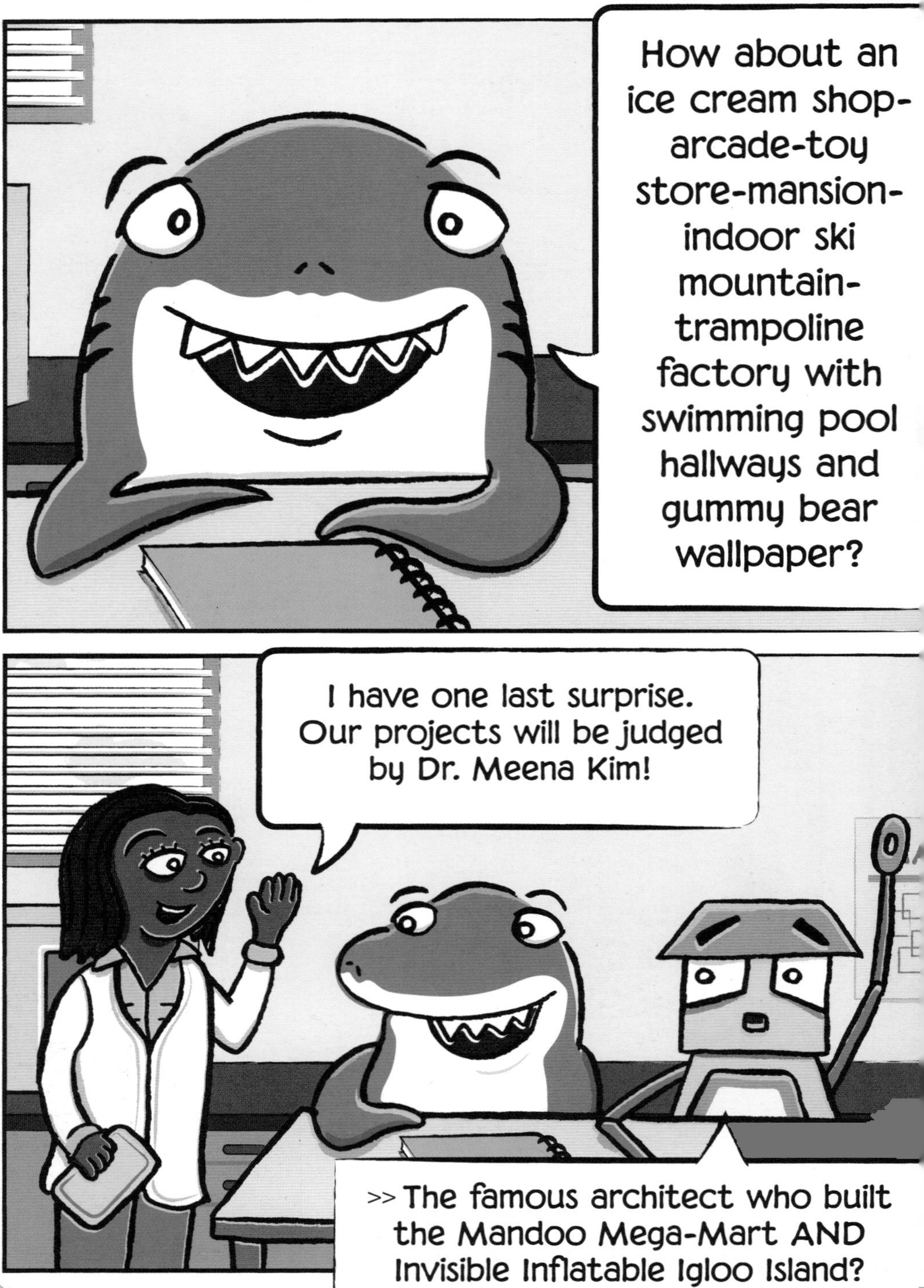
How about an ice cream shop-arcade-toy store-mansion-indoor ski mountain-trampoline factory with swimming pool hallways and gummy bear wallpaper?
I have one last surprise. Our projects will be judged by Dr. Meena Kim!
>> The famous architect who built the Mandoo Mega-Mart AND Invisible Inflatable Igloo Island?

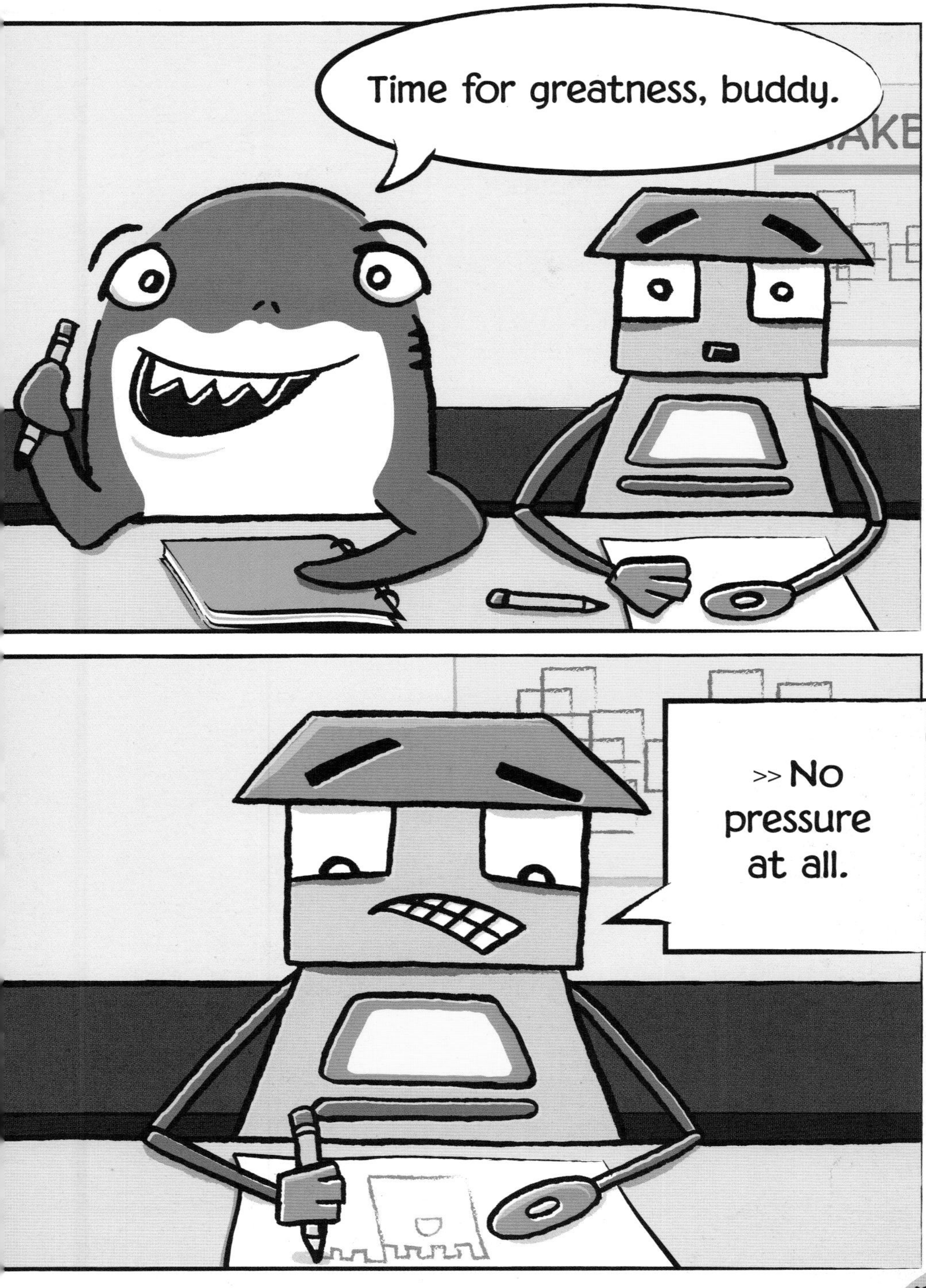
Time for greatness, buddy.
>> No pressure at all.

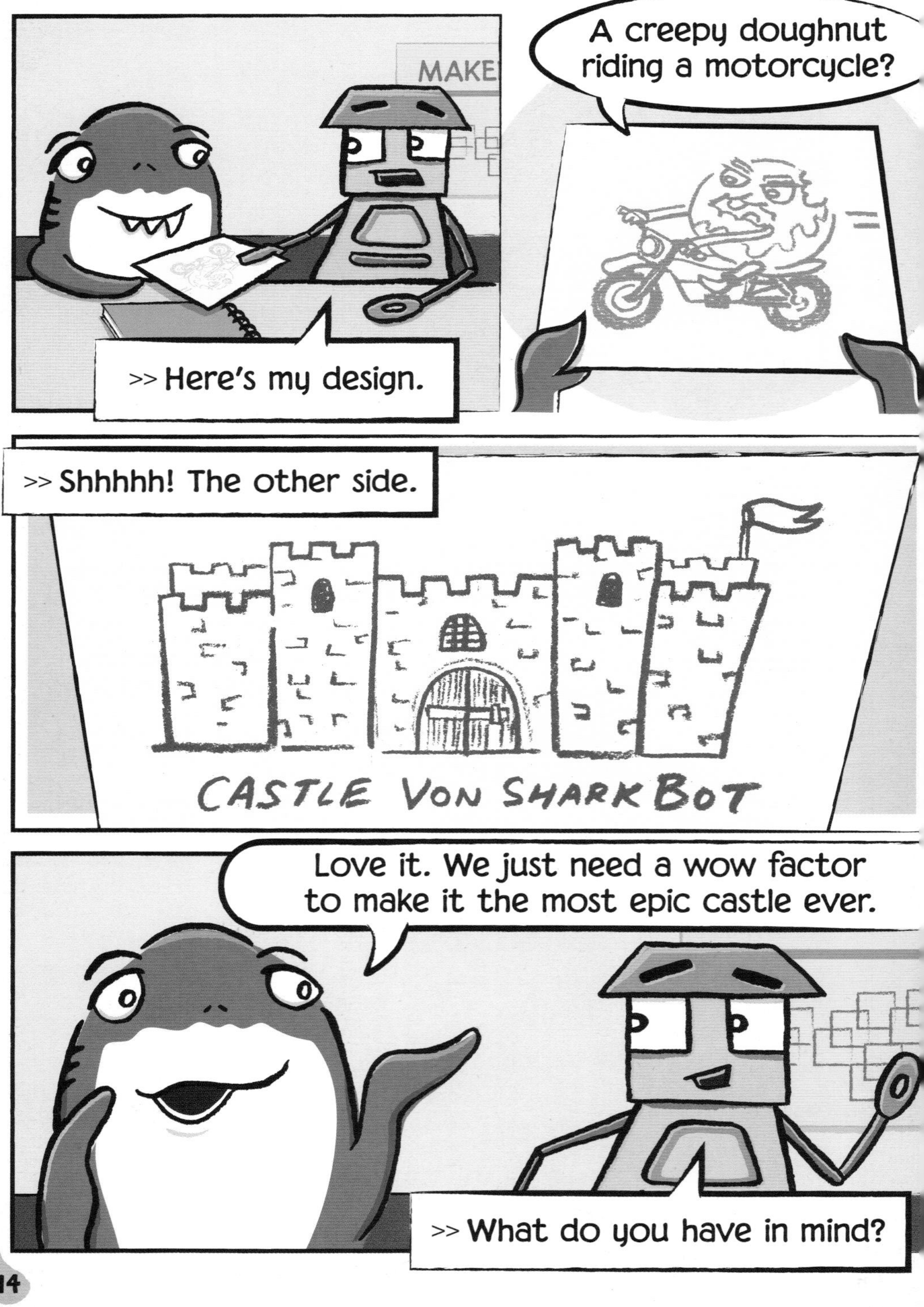
MAKE
>> Here's my design.
A creepy doughnut riding a motorcycle?
>> Shhhhh! The other side.
CASTLE VON SHARKBOT
Love it. We just need a wow factor to make it the most epic castle ever.
>> What do you have in mind?

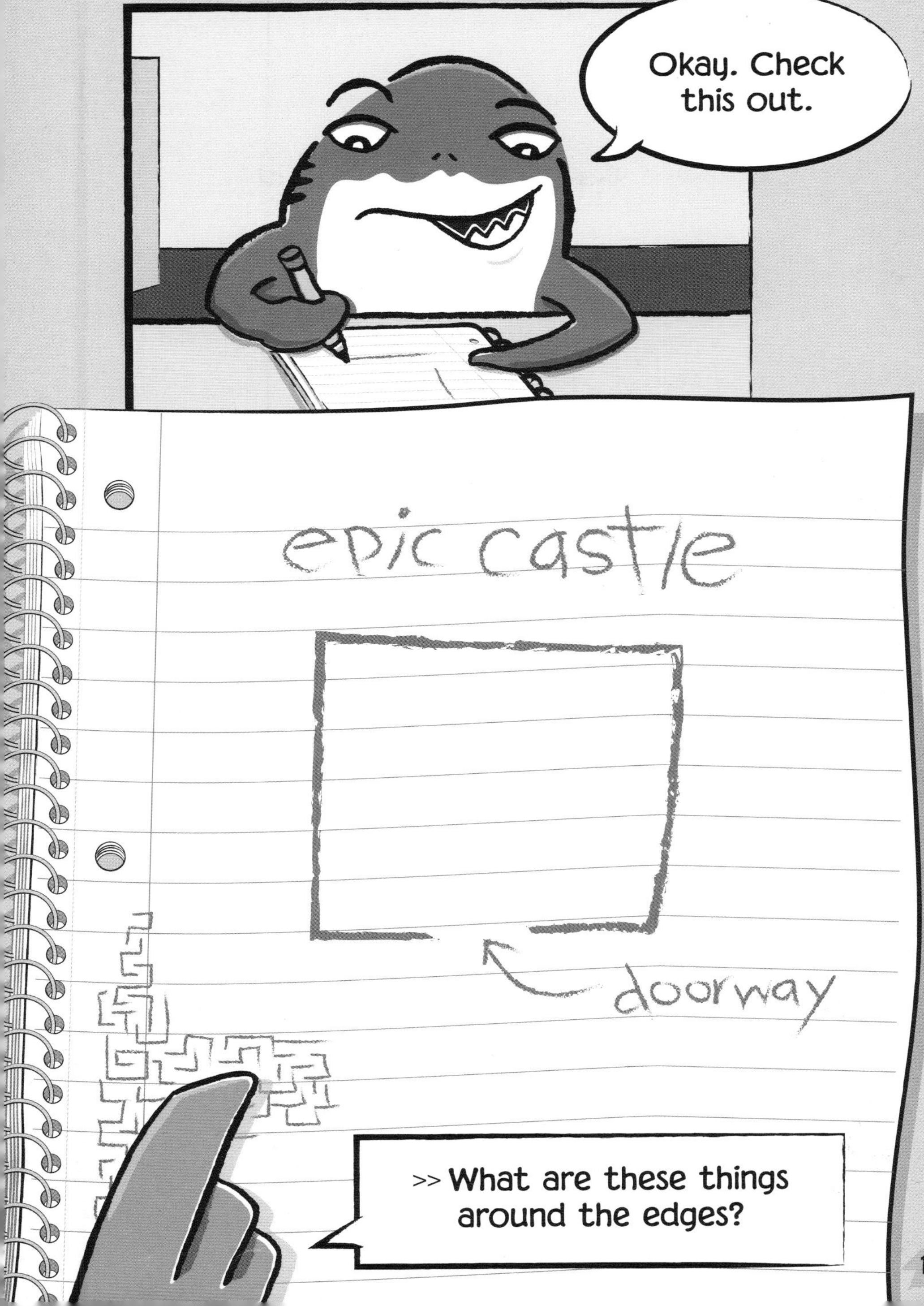
Okay. Check this out.
epic castle
doorway
>> What are these things around the edges?

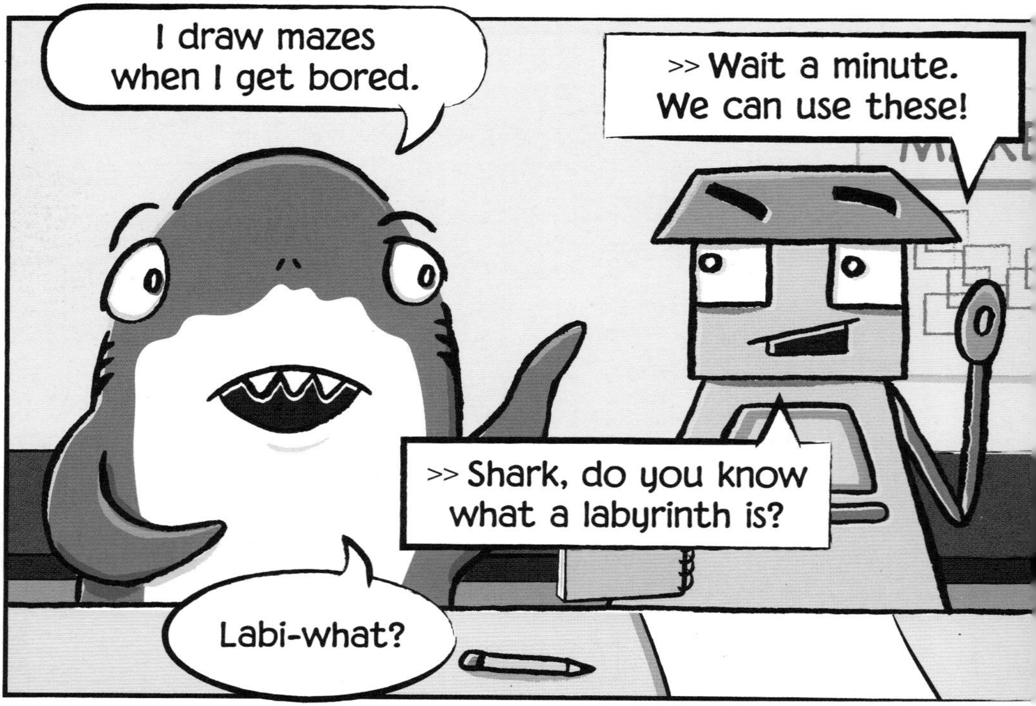
I draw mazes when I get bored.
>> Wait a minute. We can use these!
>> Shark, do you know what a labyrinth is?
Labi-what?

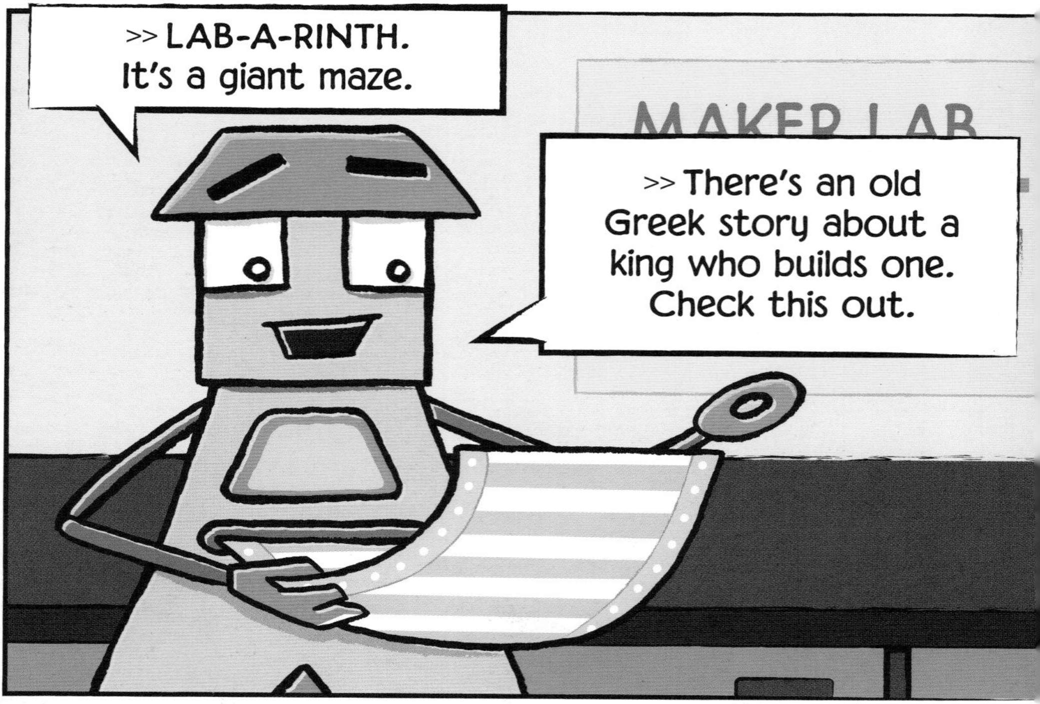
>> LAB-A-RINTH. It's a giant maze.
MAKER LAB
>> There's an old Greek story about a king who builds one. Check this out.

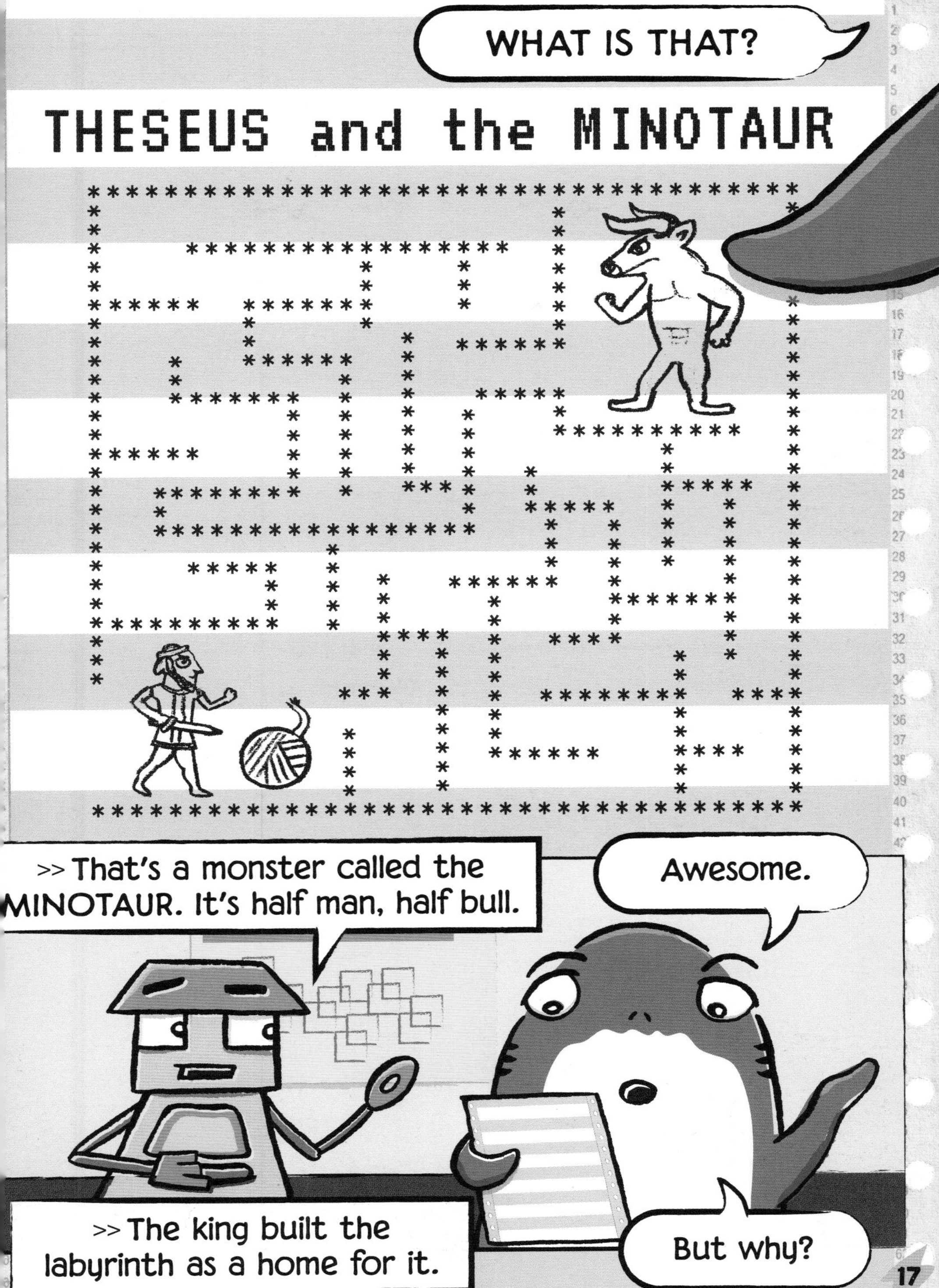
WHAT IS THAT?
THESEUS and the MINOTAUR
>> That's a monster called the MINOTAUR. It's half man, half bull.
Awesome.
>> The king built the labyrinth as a home for it.
But why?

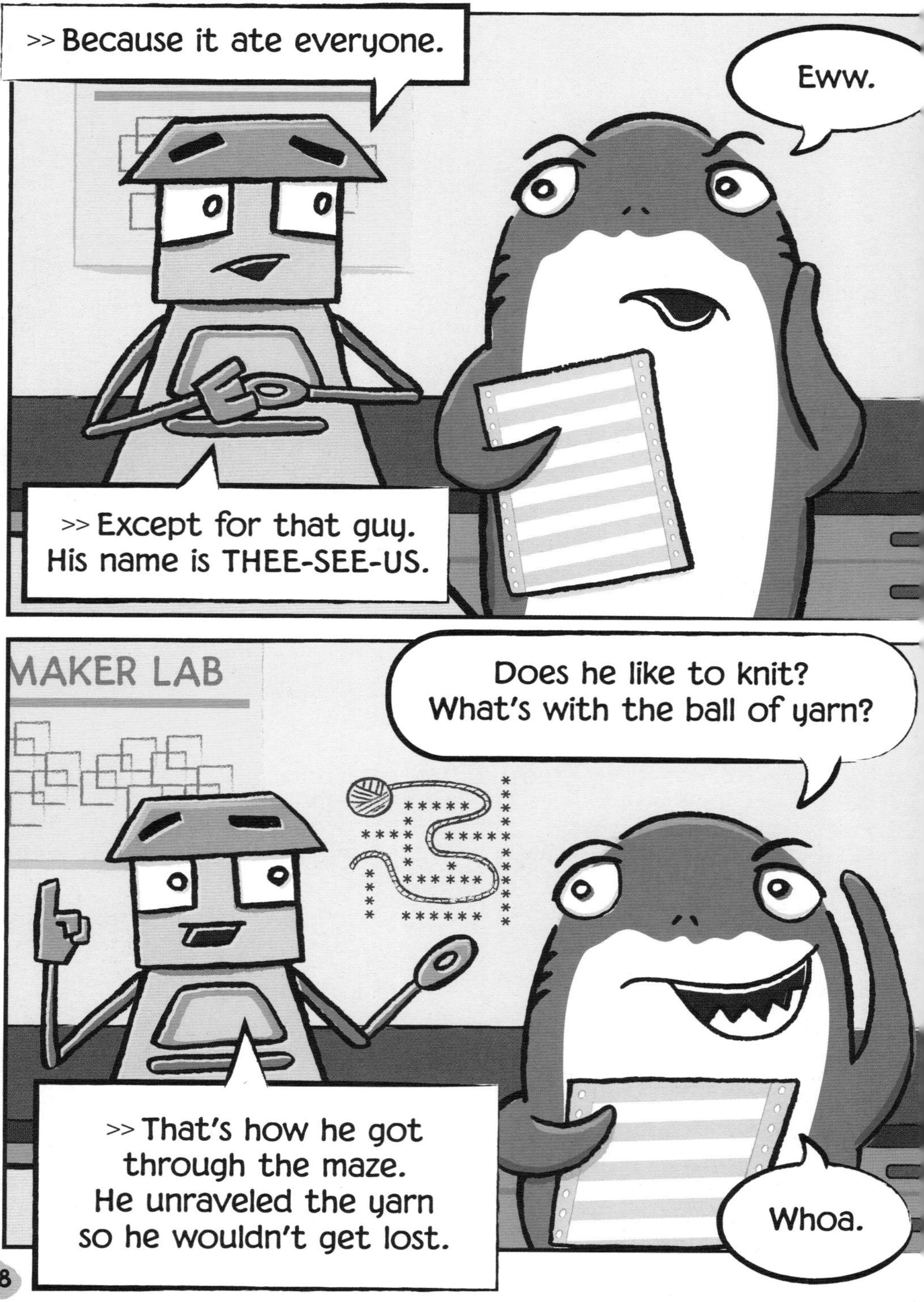
>> Because it ate everyone.
Eww.
>> Except for that guy. His name is THEE-SEE-US.
MAKER LAB
Does he like to knit? What's with the ball of yarn?
>> That's how he got through the maze. He unraveled the yarn so he wouldn't get lost.
Whoa.

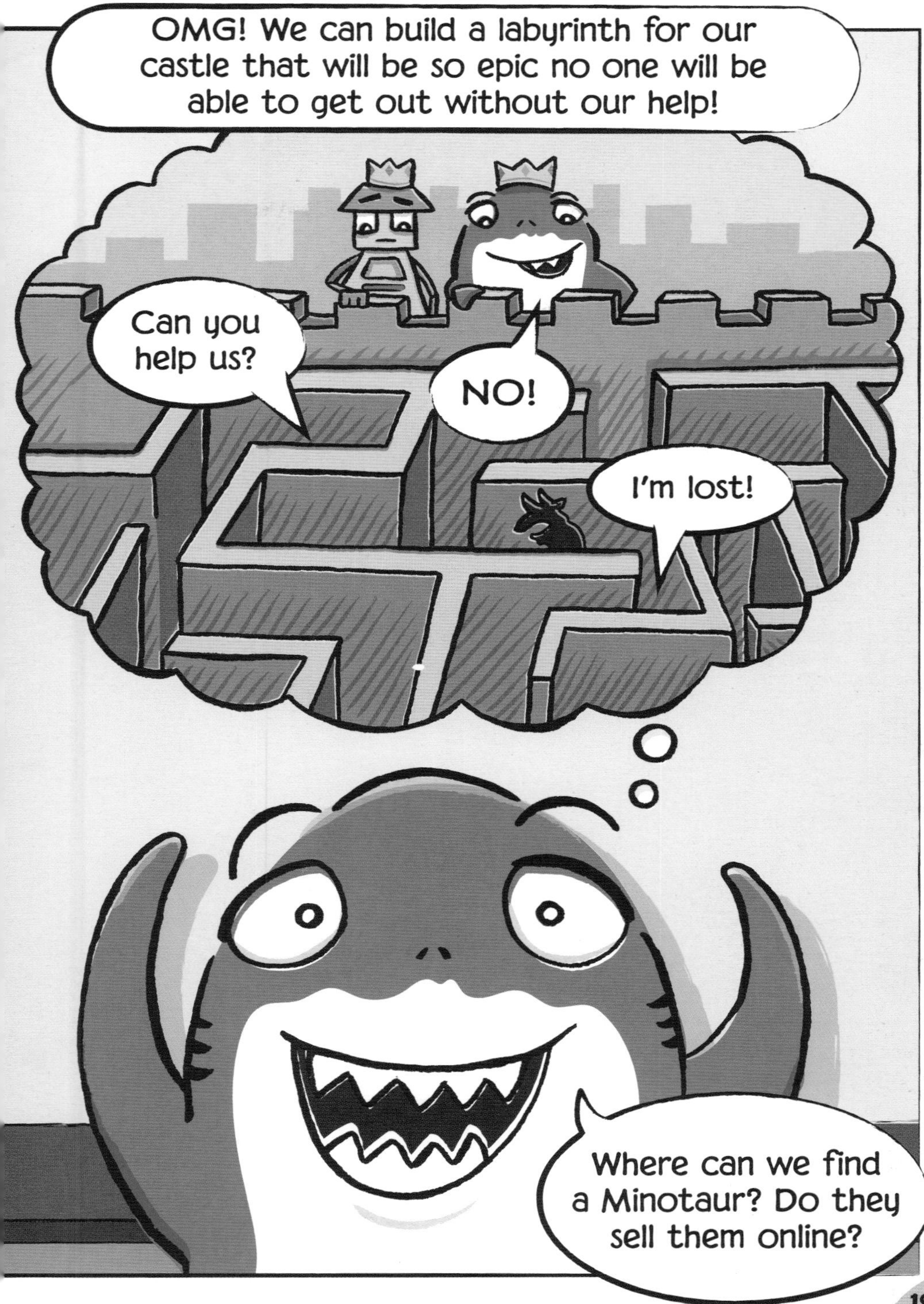
OMG! We can build a labyrinth for our castle that will be so epic no one will be able to get out without our help!
Can you help us?
NO!
I'm lost!
Where can we find a Minotaur? Do they sell them online?

Chapter 3

You Will Be A-maze-d

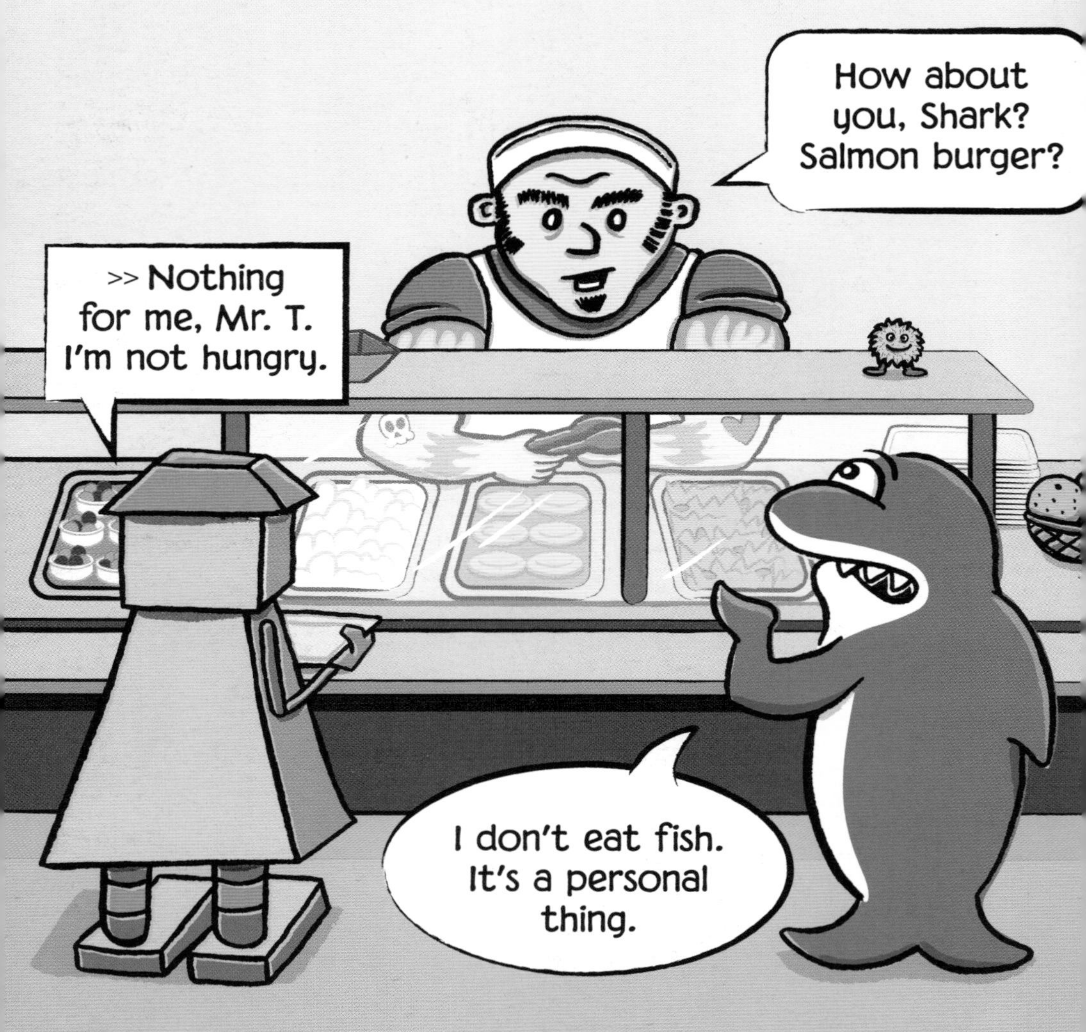
How about you, Shark? Salmon burger?
>> Nothing for me, Mr. T. I'm not hungry.
I don't eat fish. It's a personal thing.

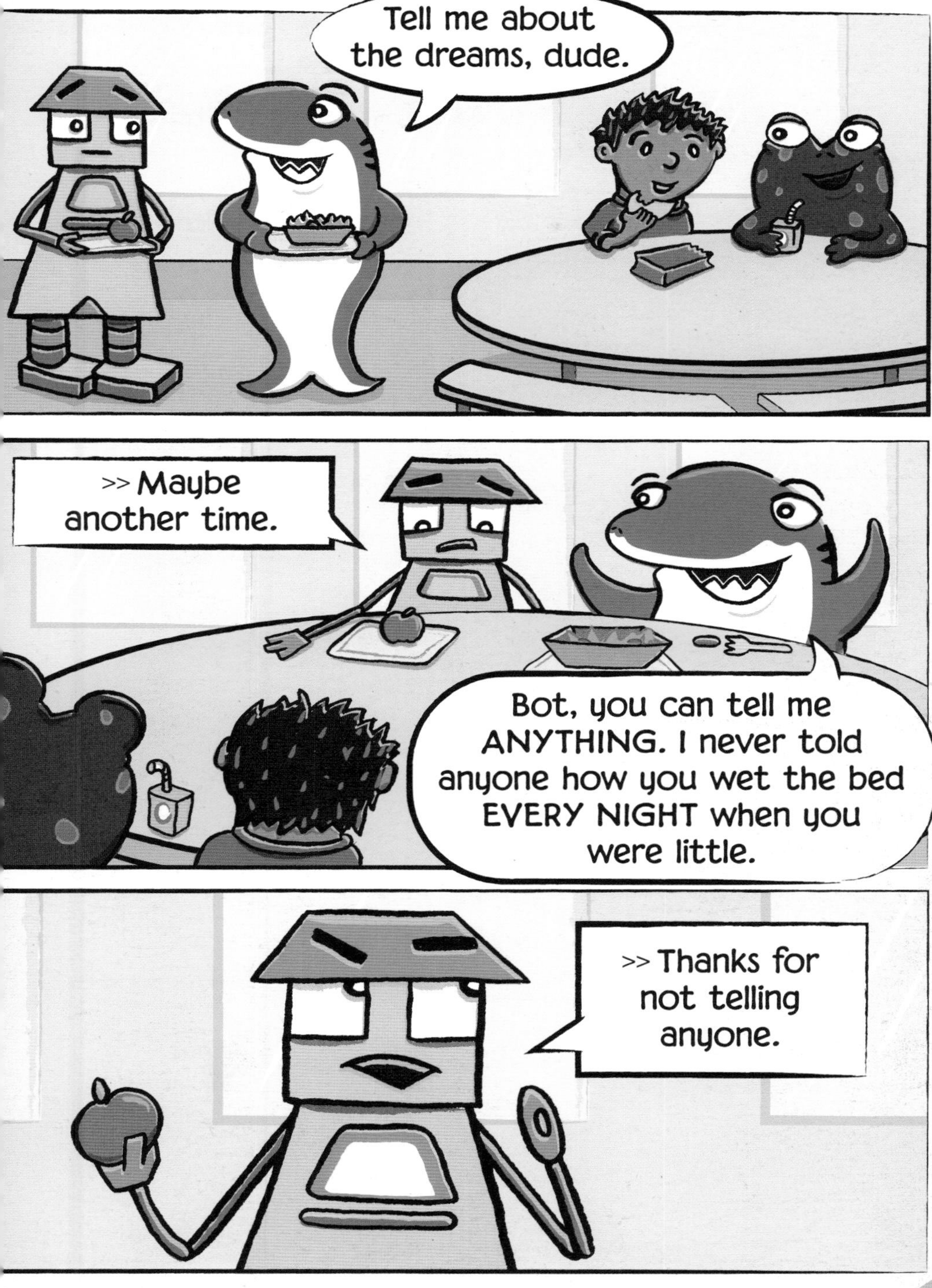
Tell me about the dreams, dude.
>> Maybe another time.
Bot, you can tell me ANYTHING. I never told anyone how you wet the bed EVERY NIGHT when you were little.
>> Thanks for not telling anyone.

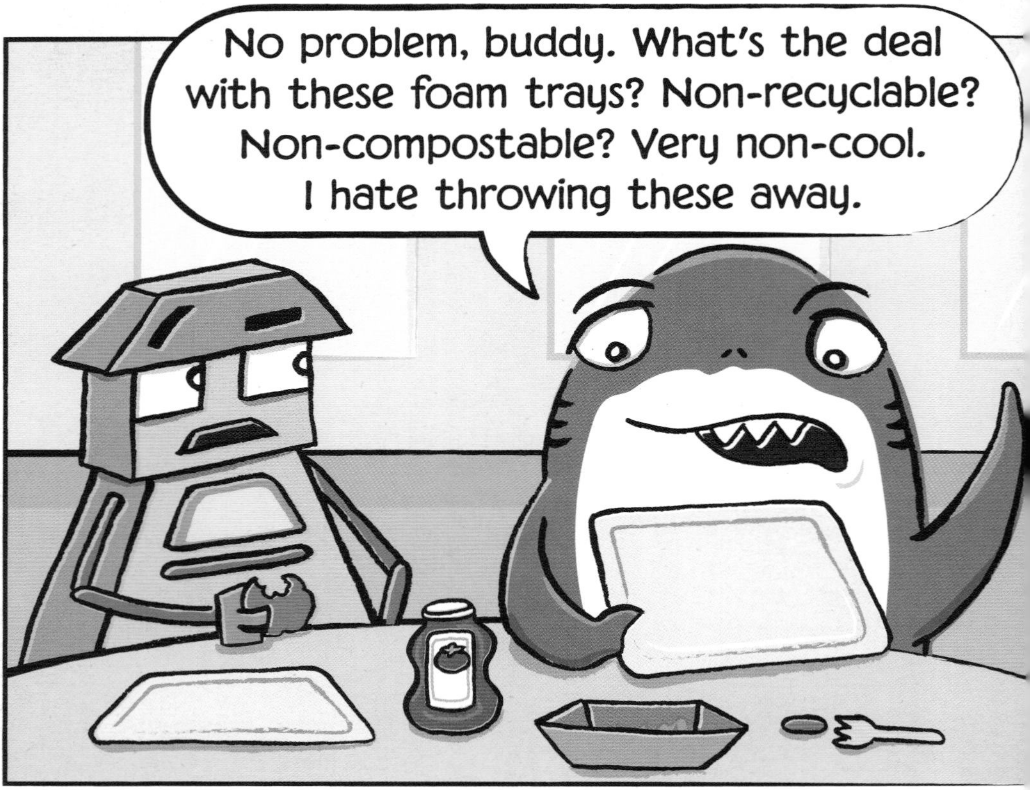
No problem, buddy. What's the deal with these foam trays? Non-recyclable? Non-compostable? Very non-cool. I hate throwing these away.

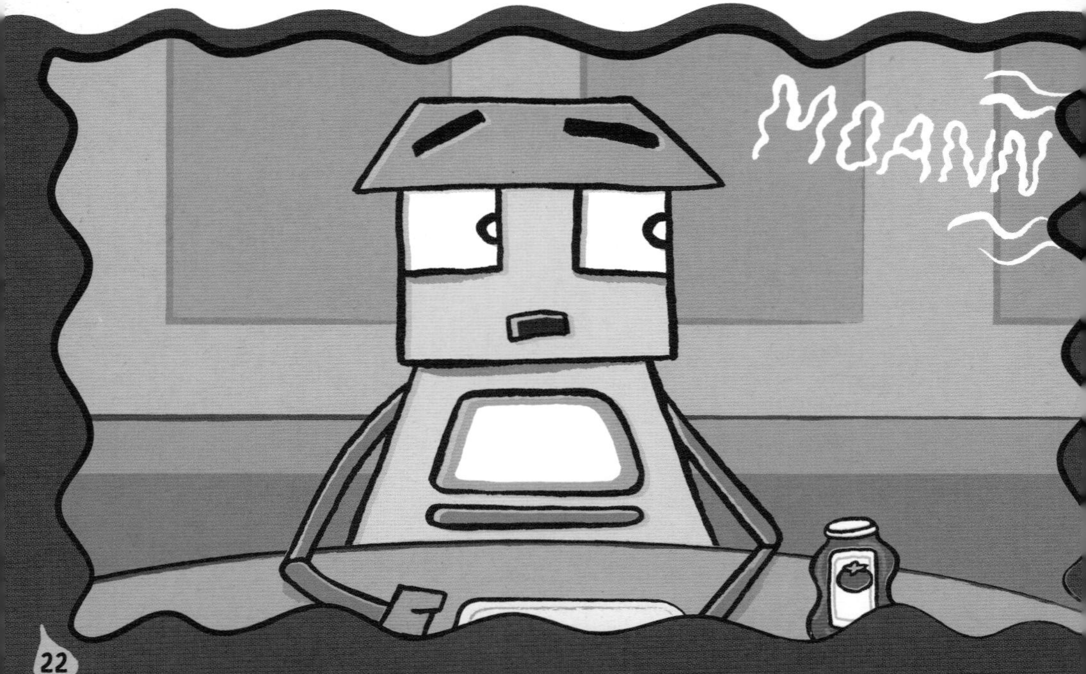
MOANN

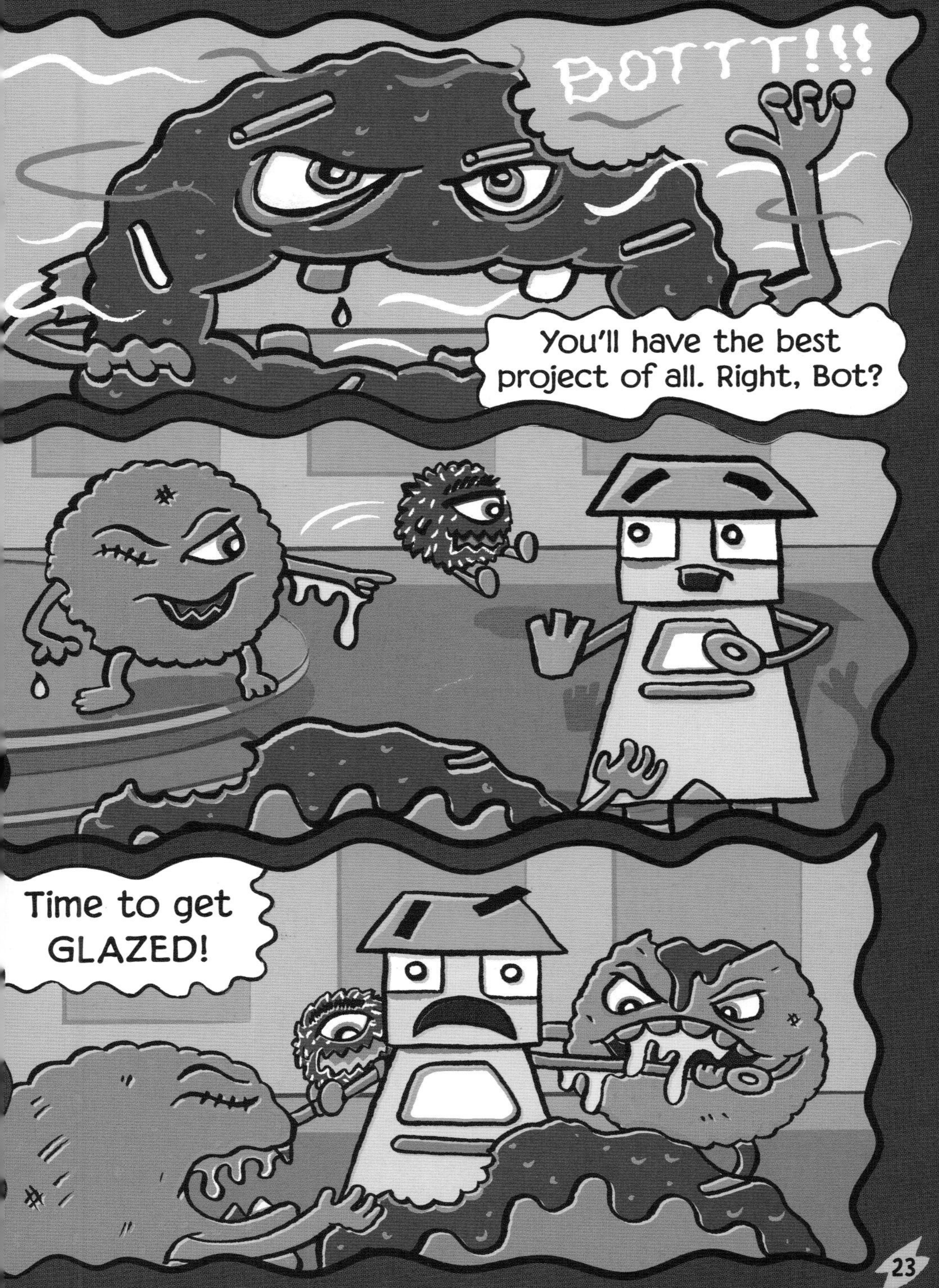
BOTTT!!!
You'll have the best project of all. Right, Bot?
Time to get GLAZED!

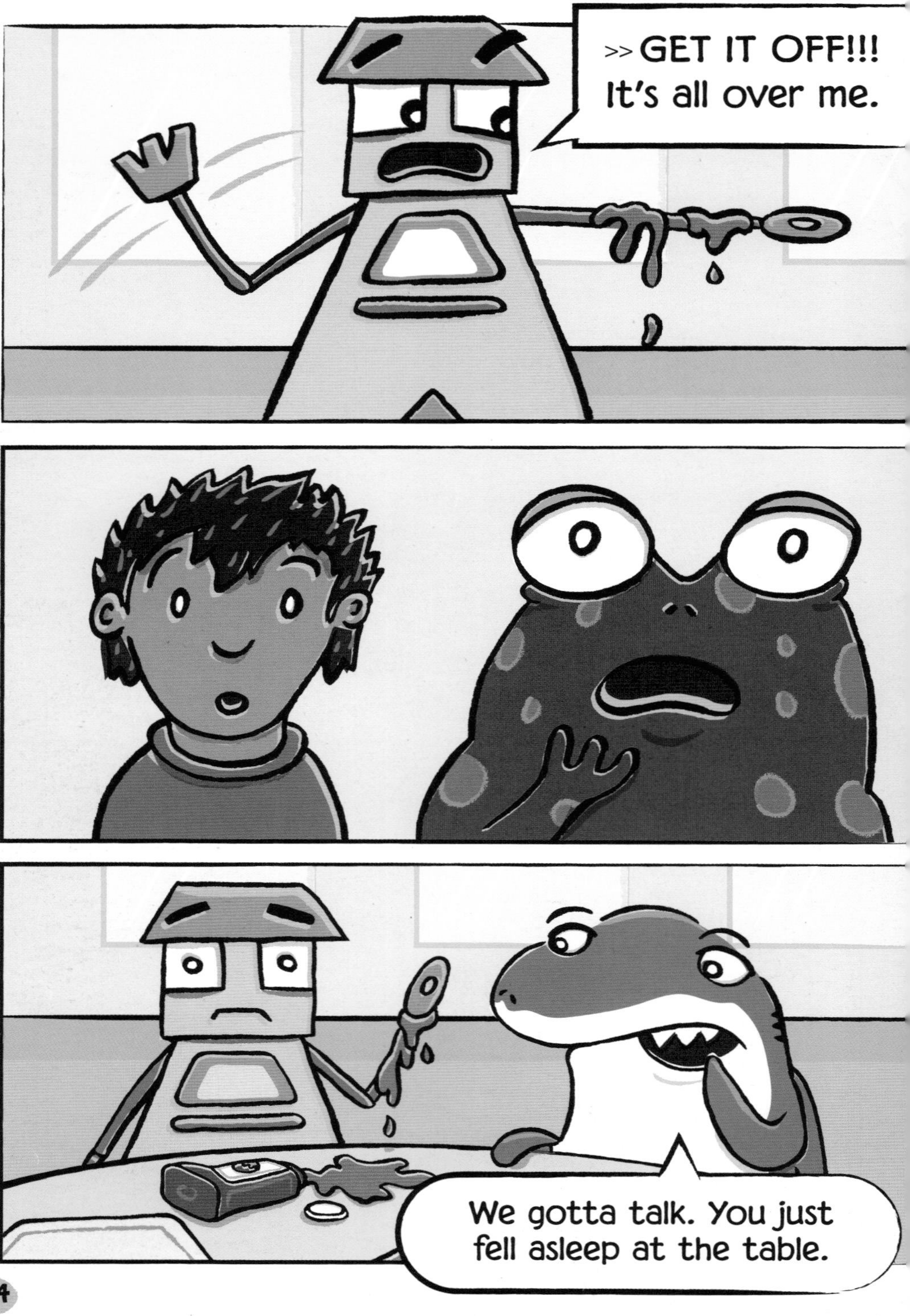
>>GET IT OFF!!! It's all over me.
We gotta talk. You just fell asleep at the table.

Chapter 4

Be Like the Water

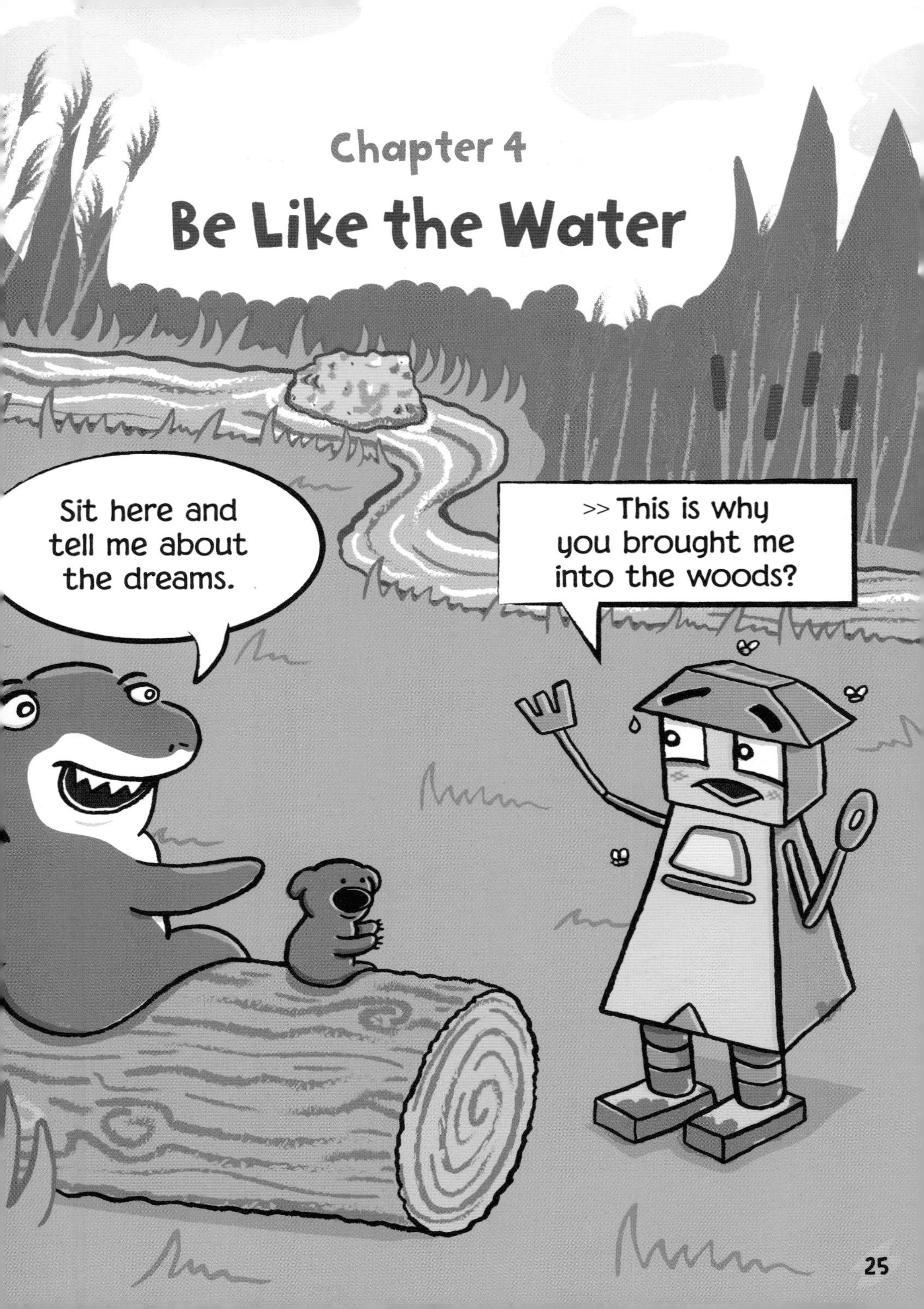
Sit here and tell me about the dreams.
>> This is why you brought me into the woods?

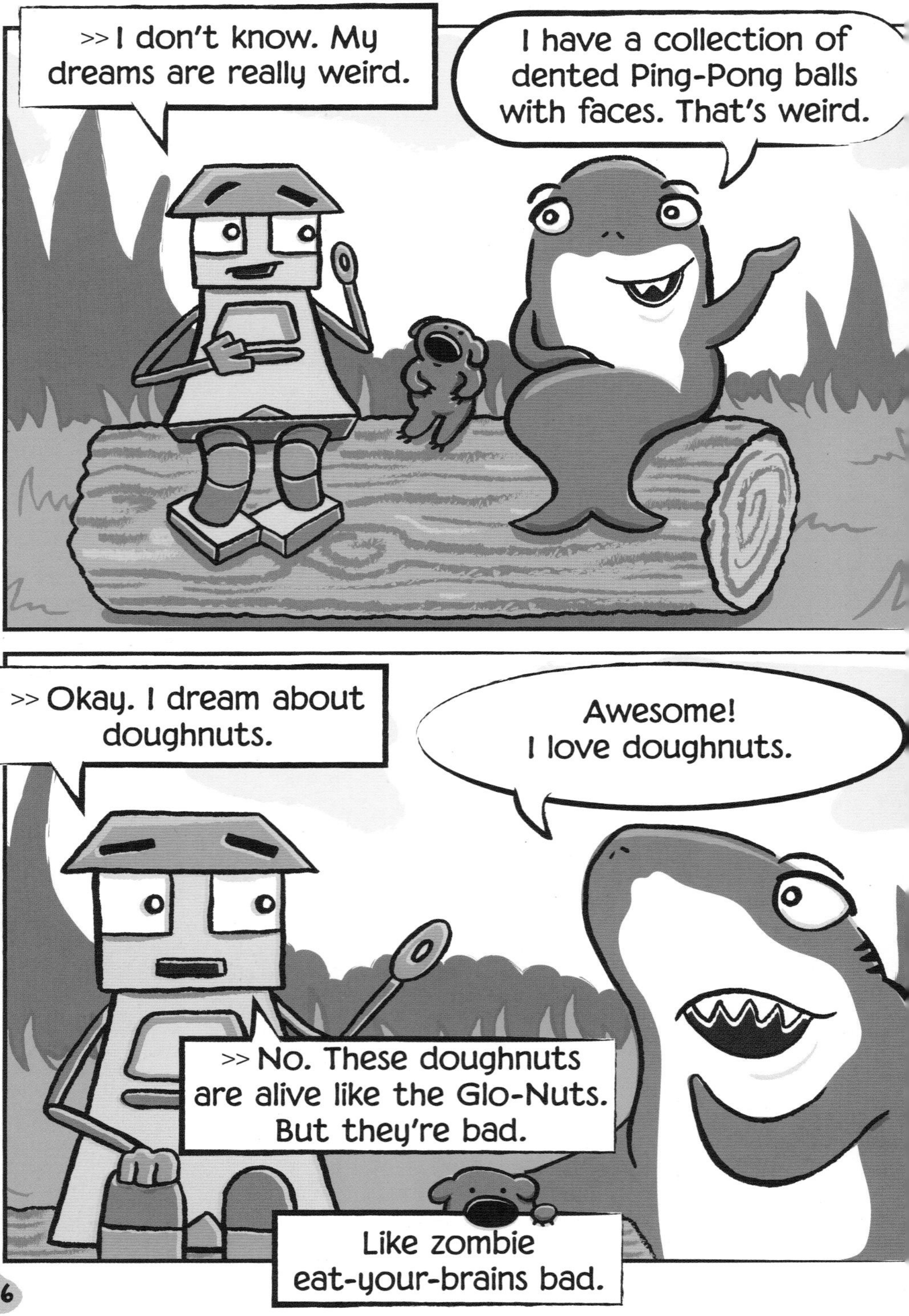
>> I don't know. My dreams are really weird.
I have a collection of dented Ping-Pong balls with faces. That's weird.
>> Okay. I dream about doughnuts.
Awesome! I love doughnuts.
>> No. These doughnuts are alive like the Glo-Nuts. But they're bad.
Like zombie eat-your-brains bad.

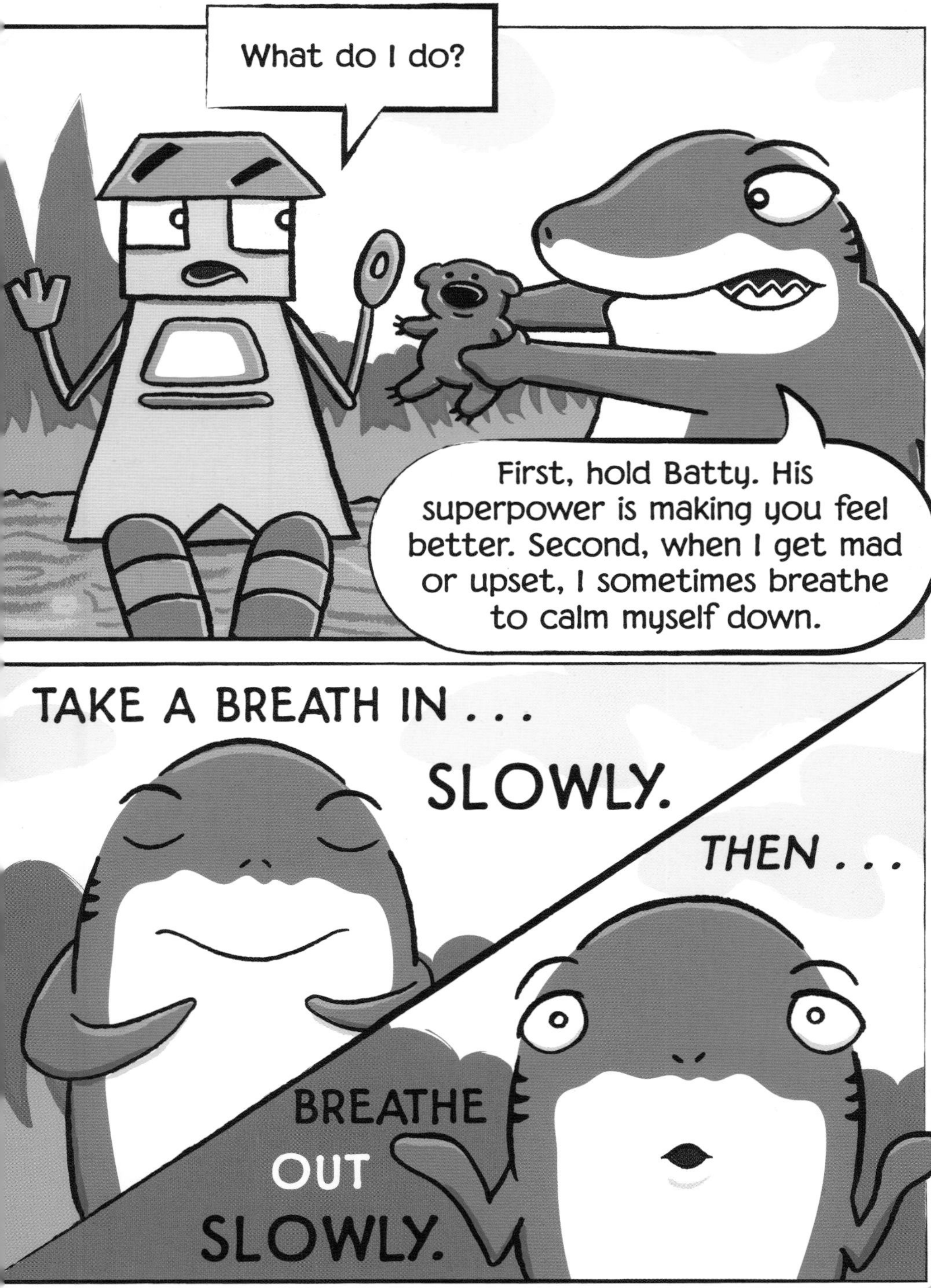

What do I do?
First, hold Batty. His superpower is making you feel better. Second, when I get mad or upset, I sometimes breathe to calm myself down.
TAKE A BREATH IN . . .
SLOWLY.
THEN . . .
BREATHE
OUT
SLOWLY.

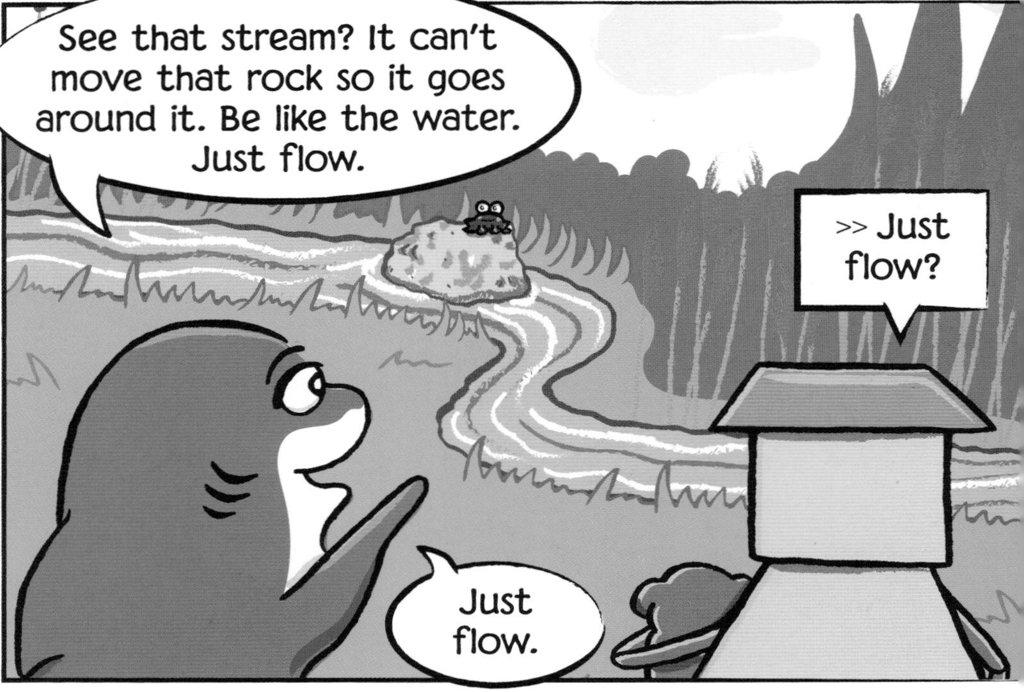
See that stream? It can't move that rock so it goes around it. Be like the water. Just flow.
>> Just flow?
Just flow.

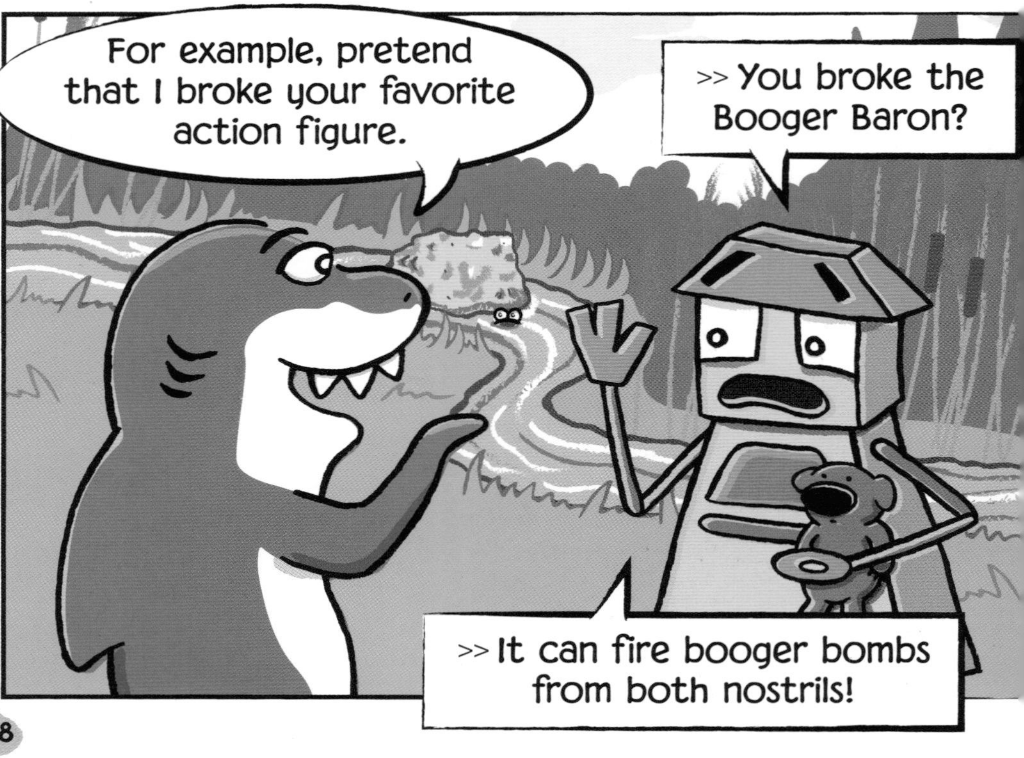
For example, pretend that I broke your favorite action figure.
>> You broke the Booger Baron?
>> It can fire booger bombs from both nostrils!

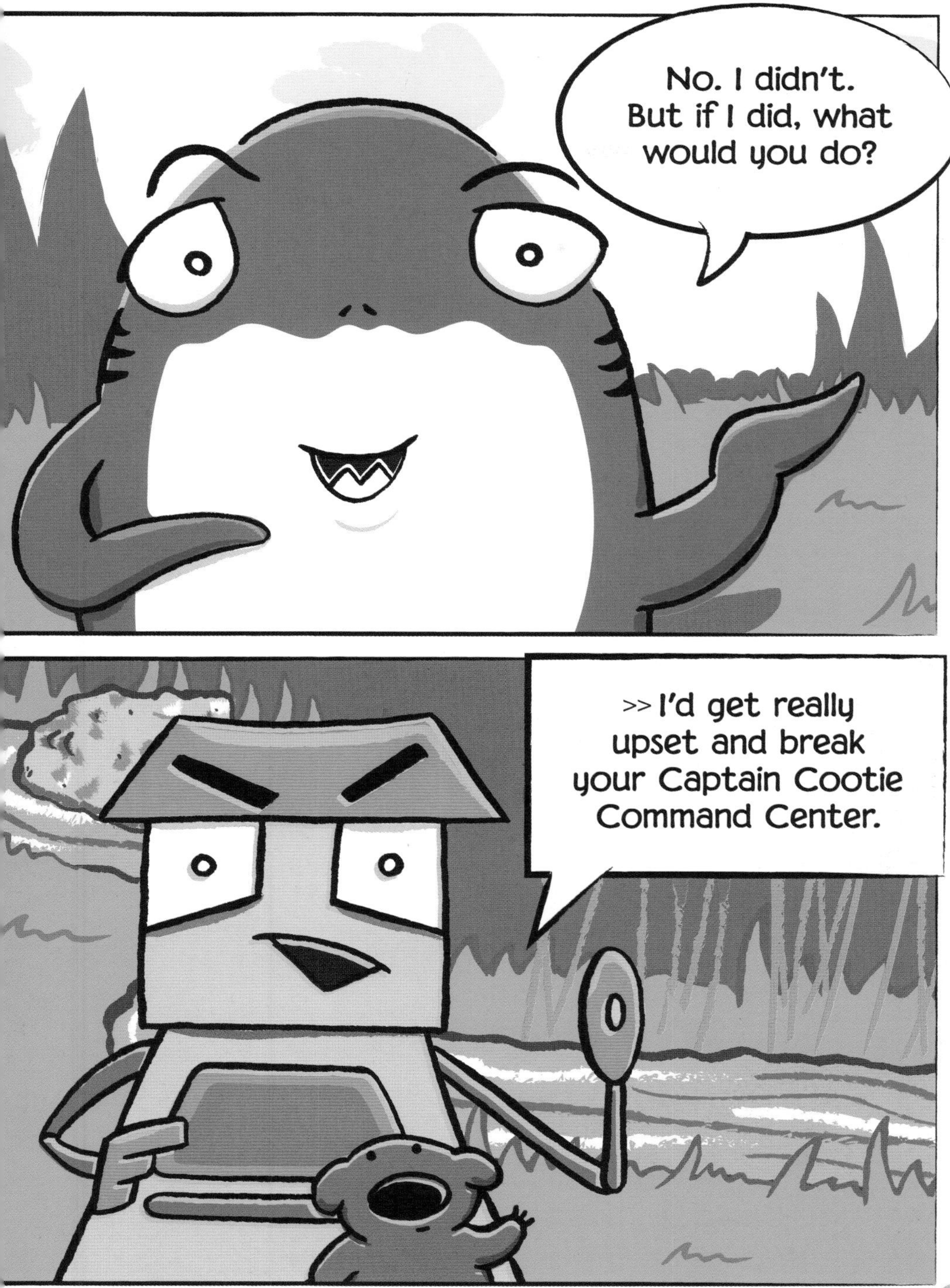
No. I didn't. But if I did, what would you do?
>> I'd get really upset and break your Captain Cootie Command Center.

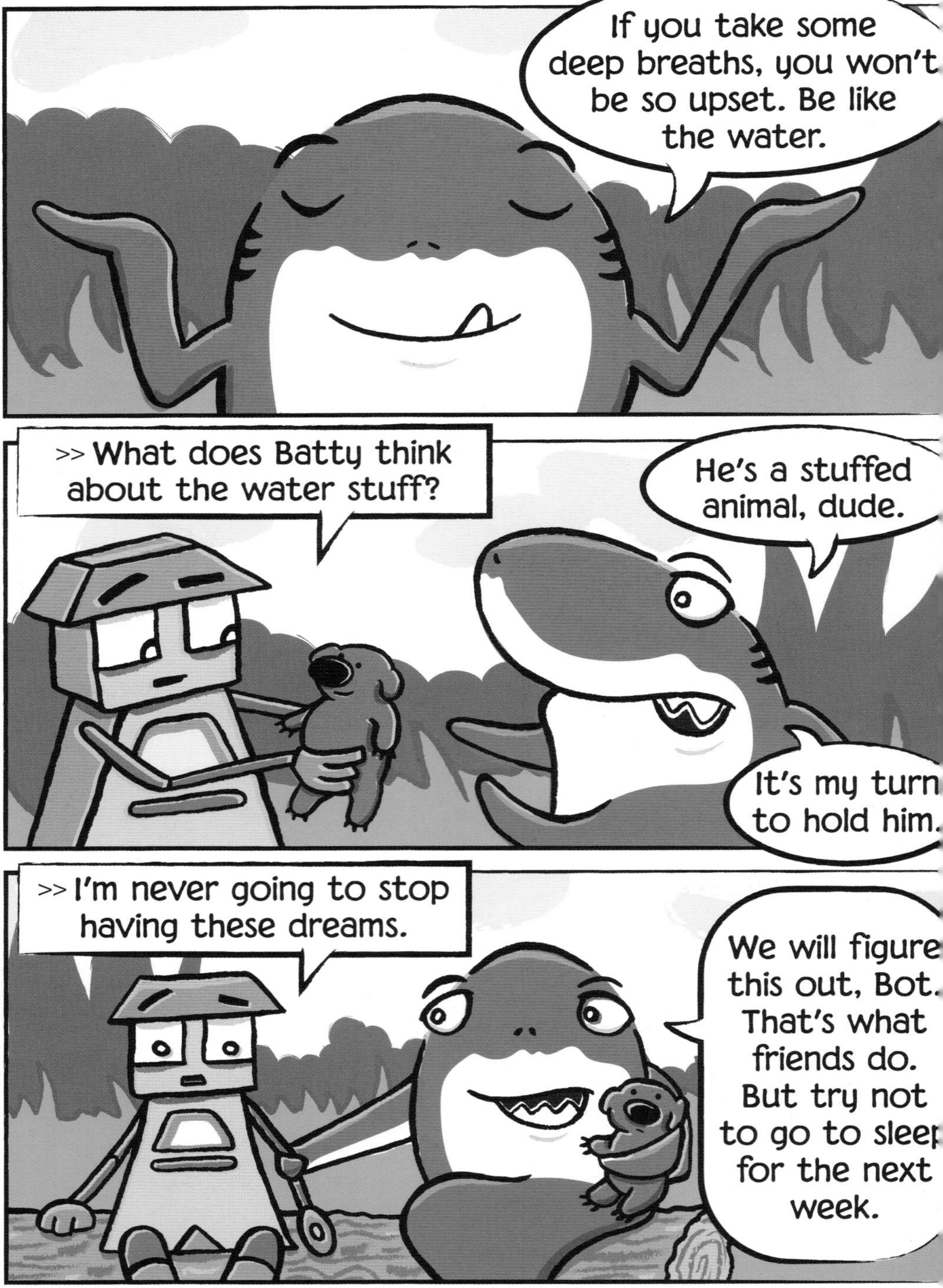
If you take some deep breaths, you won't be so upset. Be like the water.
>> What does Batty think about the water stuff?
He's a stuffed animal, dude.
It's my turn to hold him.
>> I'm never going to stop having these dreams.
We will figure this out, Bot. That's what friends do. But try not to go to sleep for the next week.

Chapter 5

All of Them?

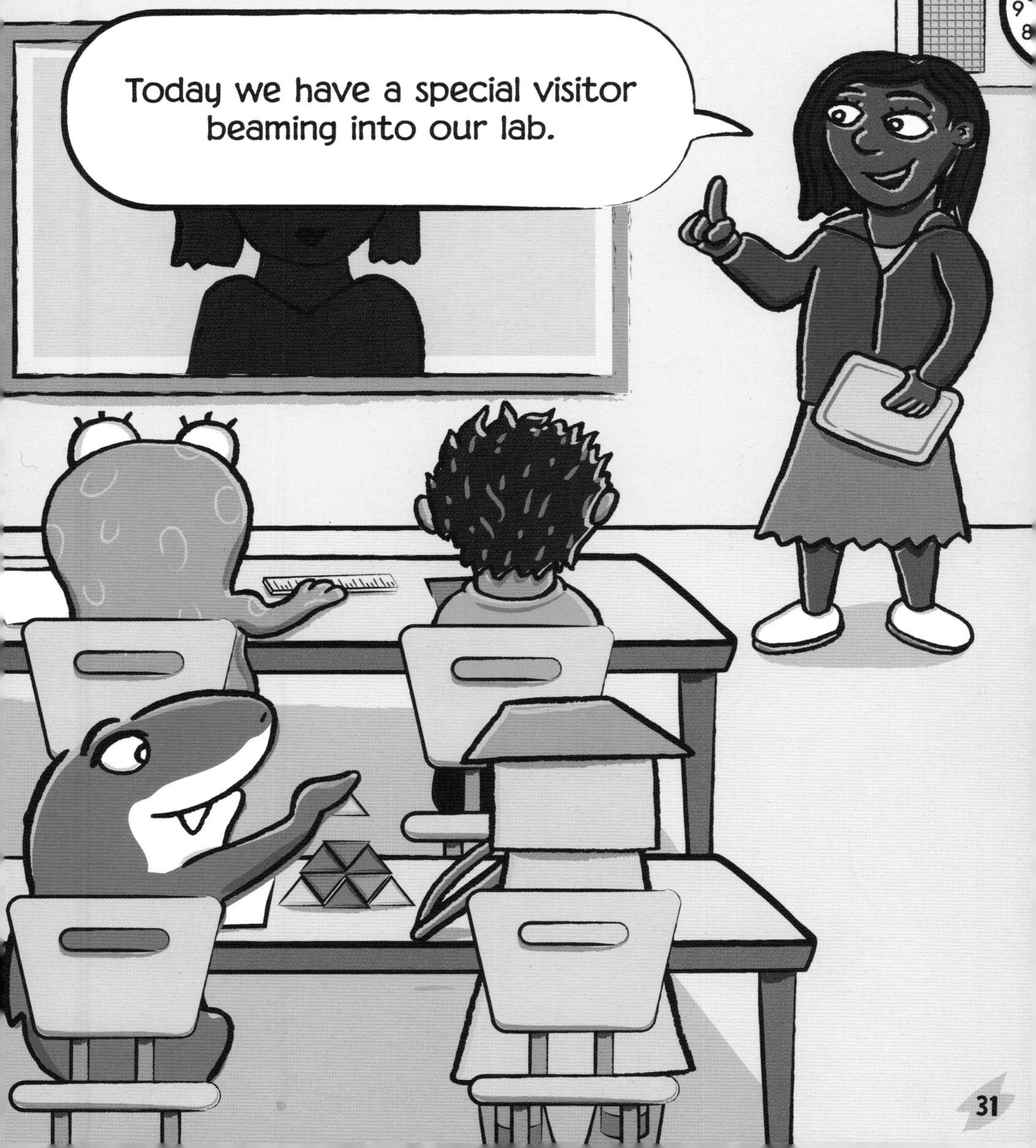

Today we have a special visitor beaming into our lab.

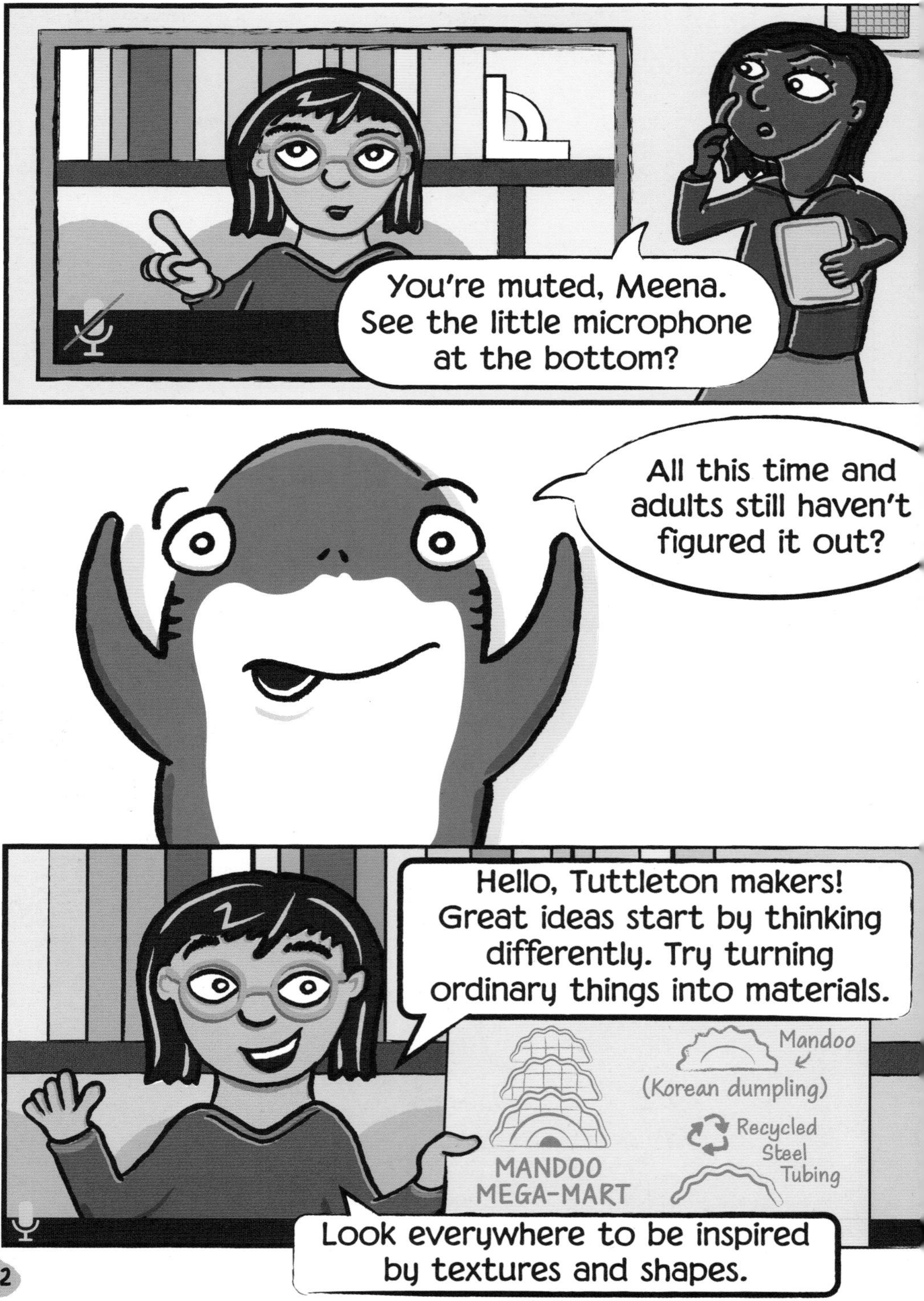
You're muted, Meena. See the little microphone at the bottom?
All this time and adults still haven't figured it out?
Hello, Tuttleton makers! Great ideas start by thinking differently. Try turning ordinary things into materials.
Mandoo
(Korean dumpling)
Recycled Steel Tubing
MANDOO MEGA-MART
Look everywhere to be inspired by textures and shapes.

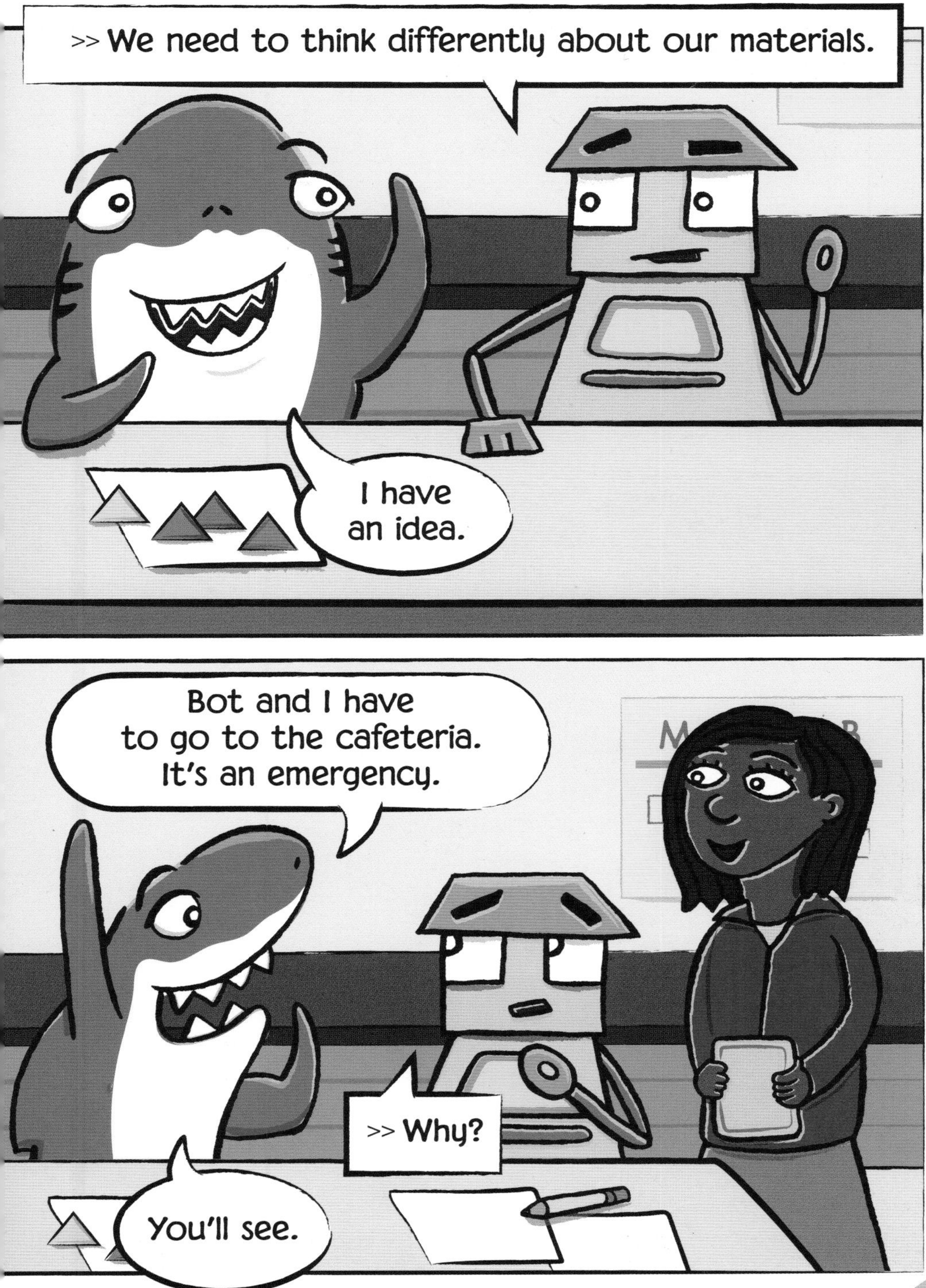

>> We need to think differently about our materials.
I have an idea.
Bot and I have to go to the cafeteria. It's an emergency.
>> Why?
You'll see.

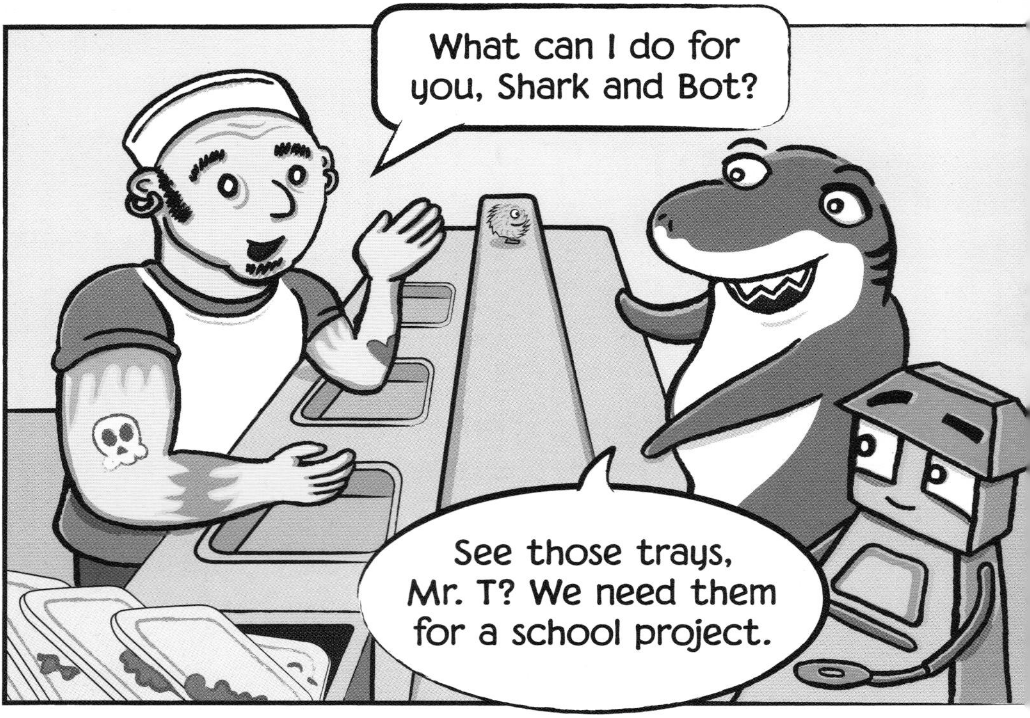
What can I do for you, Shark and Bot?
See those trays, Mr. T? We need them for a school project.

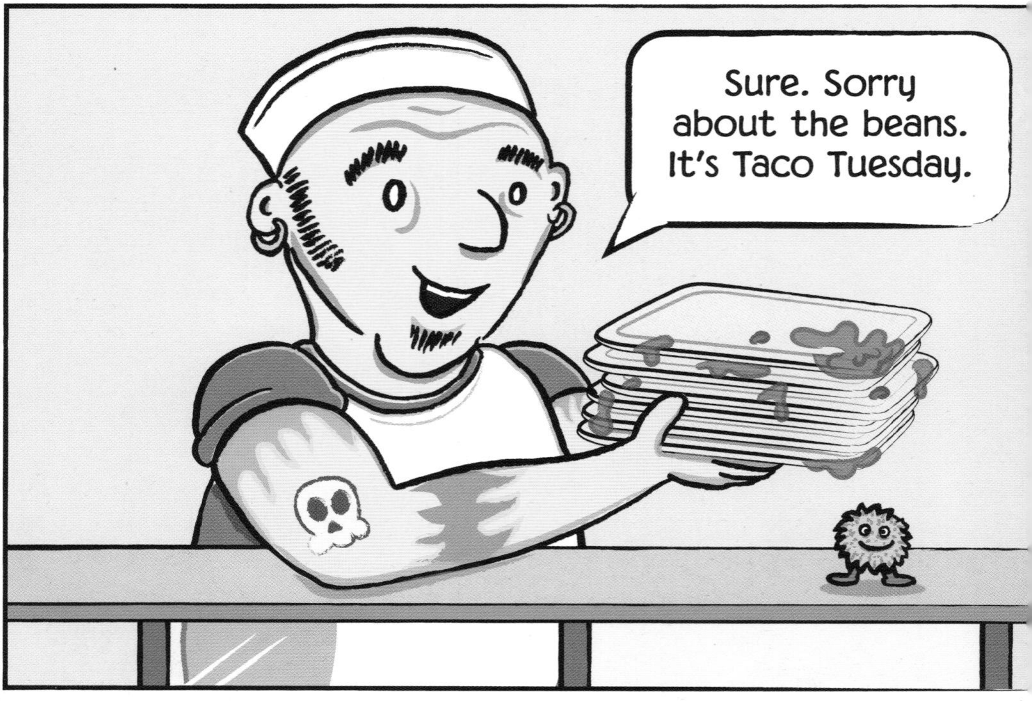
Sure. Sorry about the beans. It's Taco Tuesday.

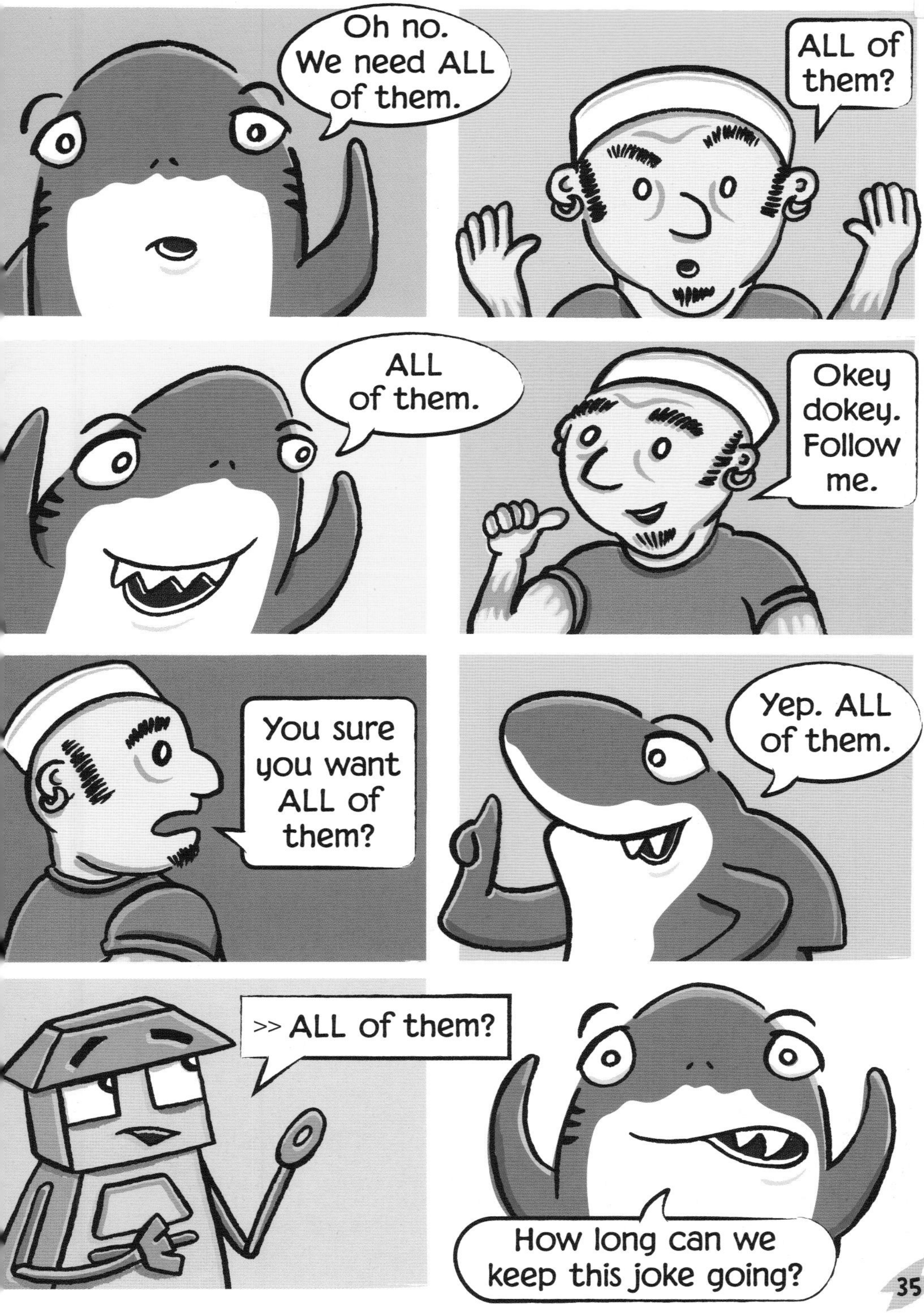
Oh no. We need ALL of them.
ALL of them?
ALL of them.
Okey dokey. Follow me.
You sure you want ALL of them?
Yep. ALL of them.
>> ALL of them?
How long can we keep this joke going?

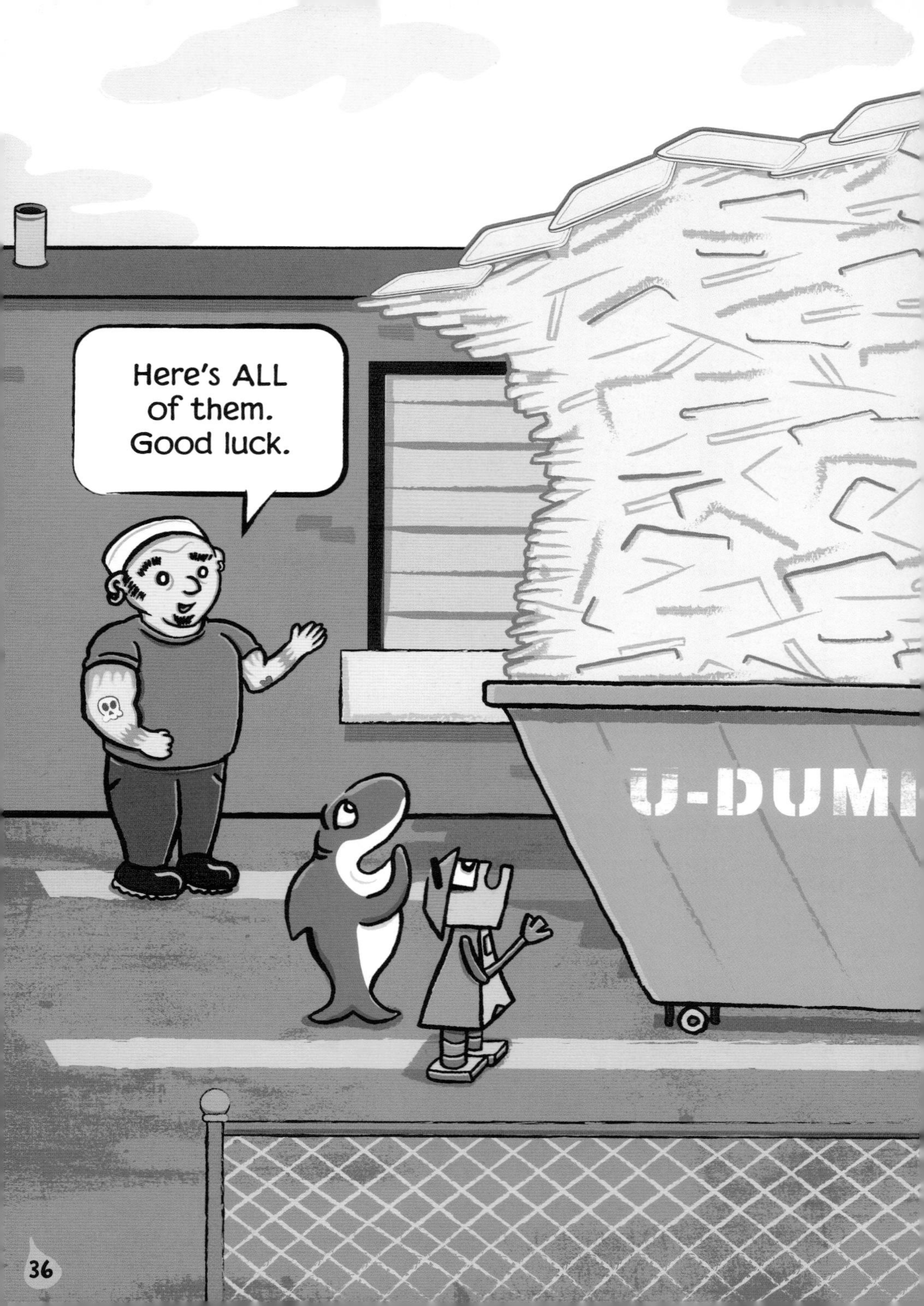
Here's ALL of them. Good luck.
U-DUMP

Chapter 6

Build-o-rama

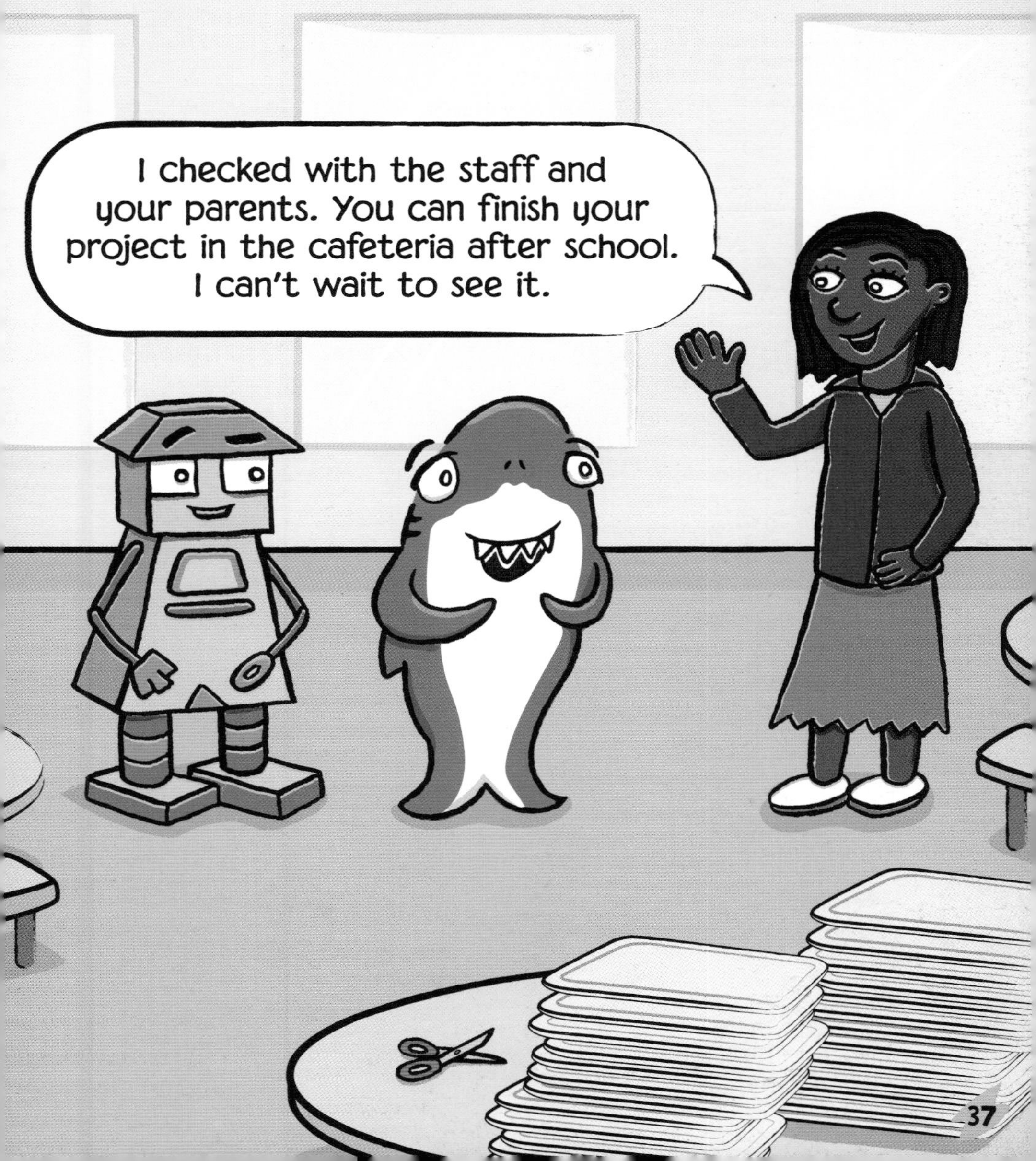
I checked with the staff and your parents. You can finish your project in the cafeteria after school. I can't wait to see it.

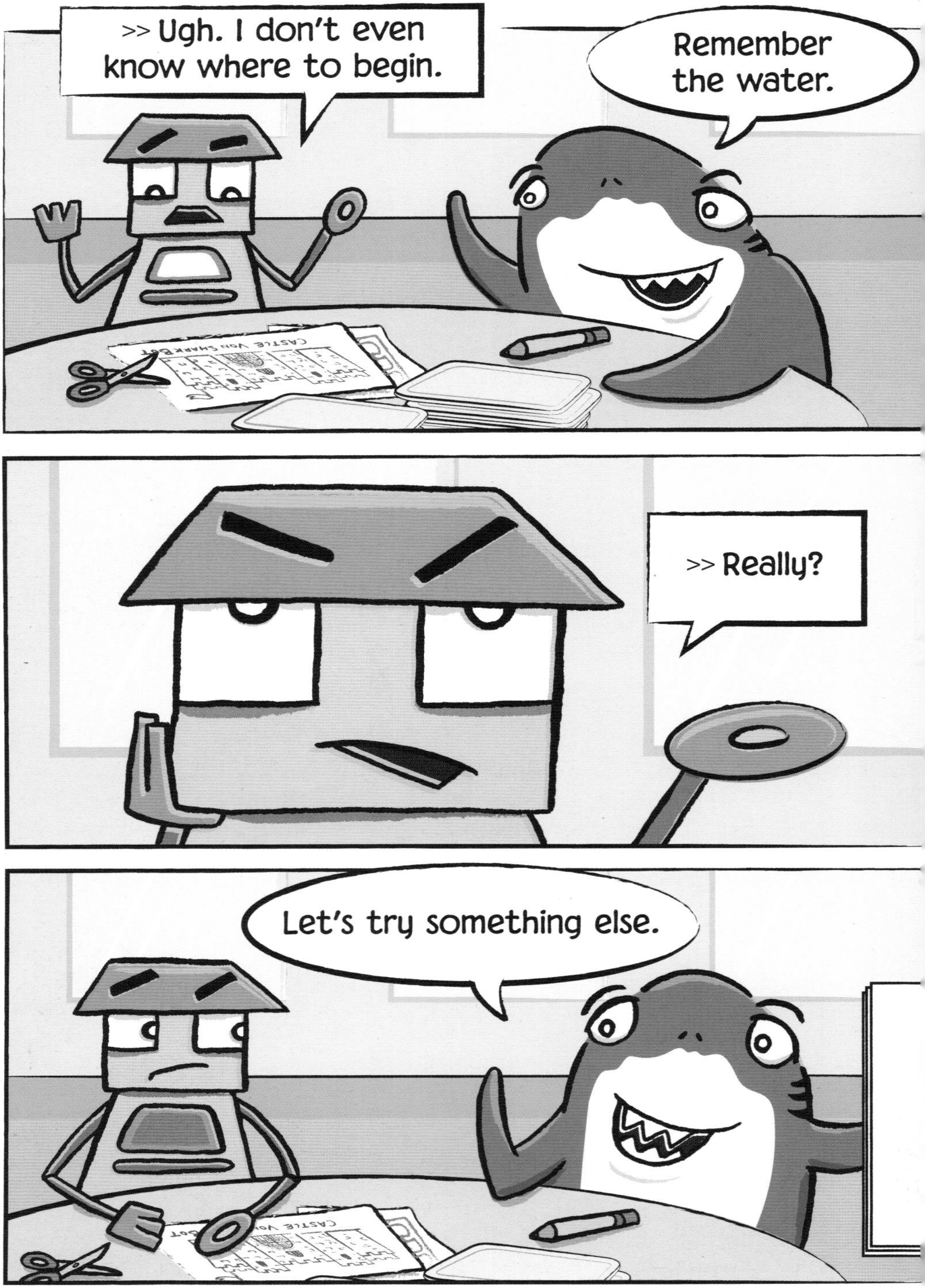
>> Ugh. I don't even know where to begin.
Remember the water.
>> Really?
Let's try something else.

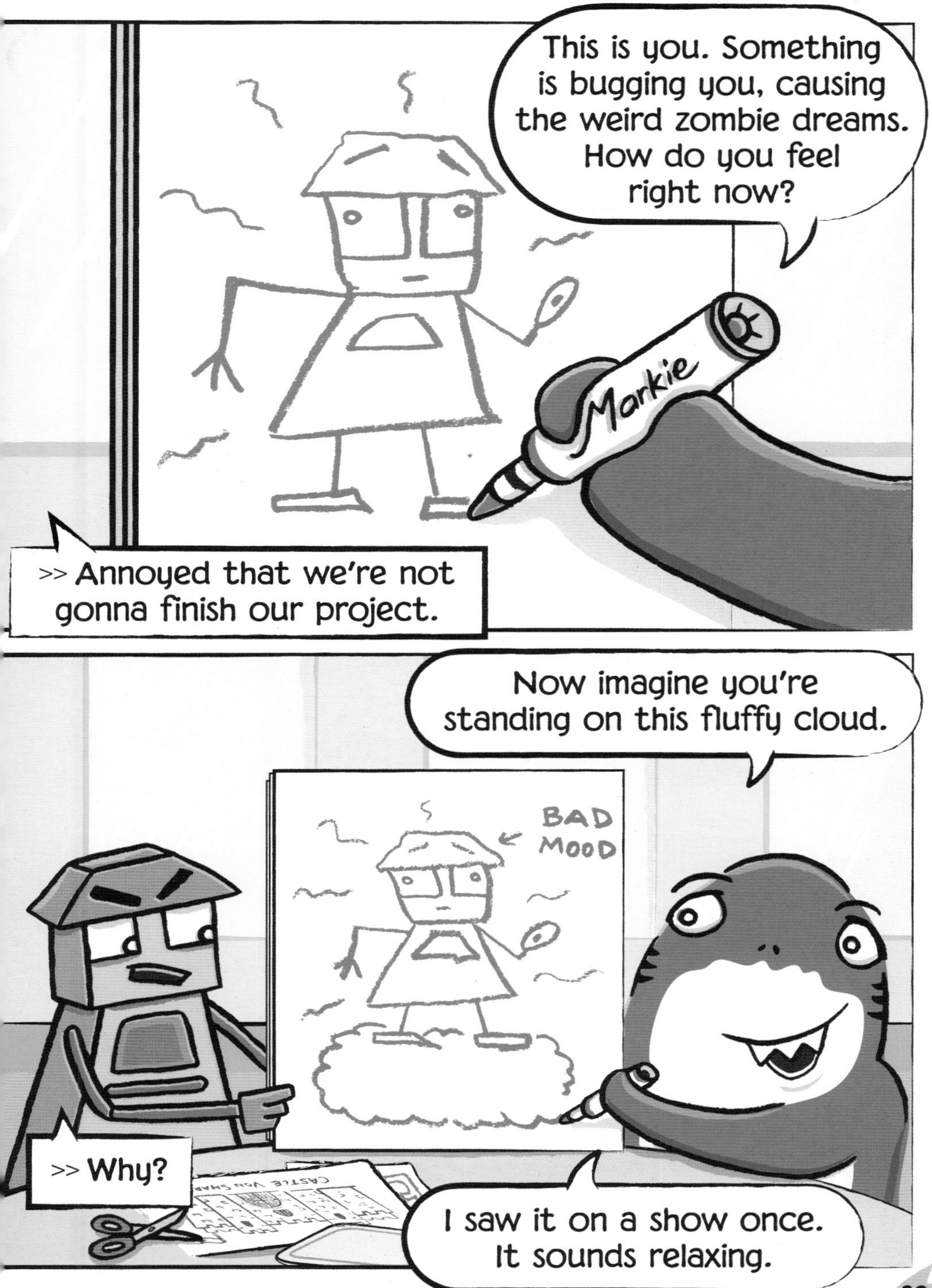
This is you. Something is bugging you, causing the weird zombie dreams. How do you feel right now?
Markie
>> Annoyed that we're not gonna finish our project.
Now imagine you're standing on this fluffy cloud.
BAD MOOD
>> Why?
I saw it on a show once. It sounds relaxing.

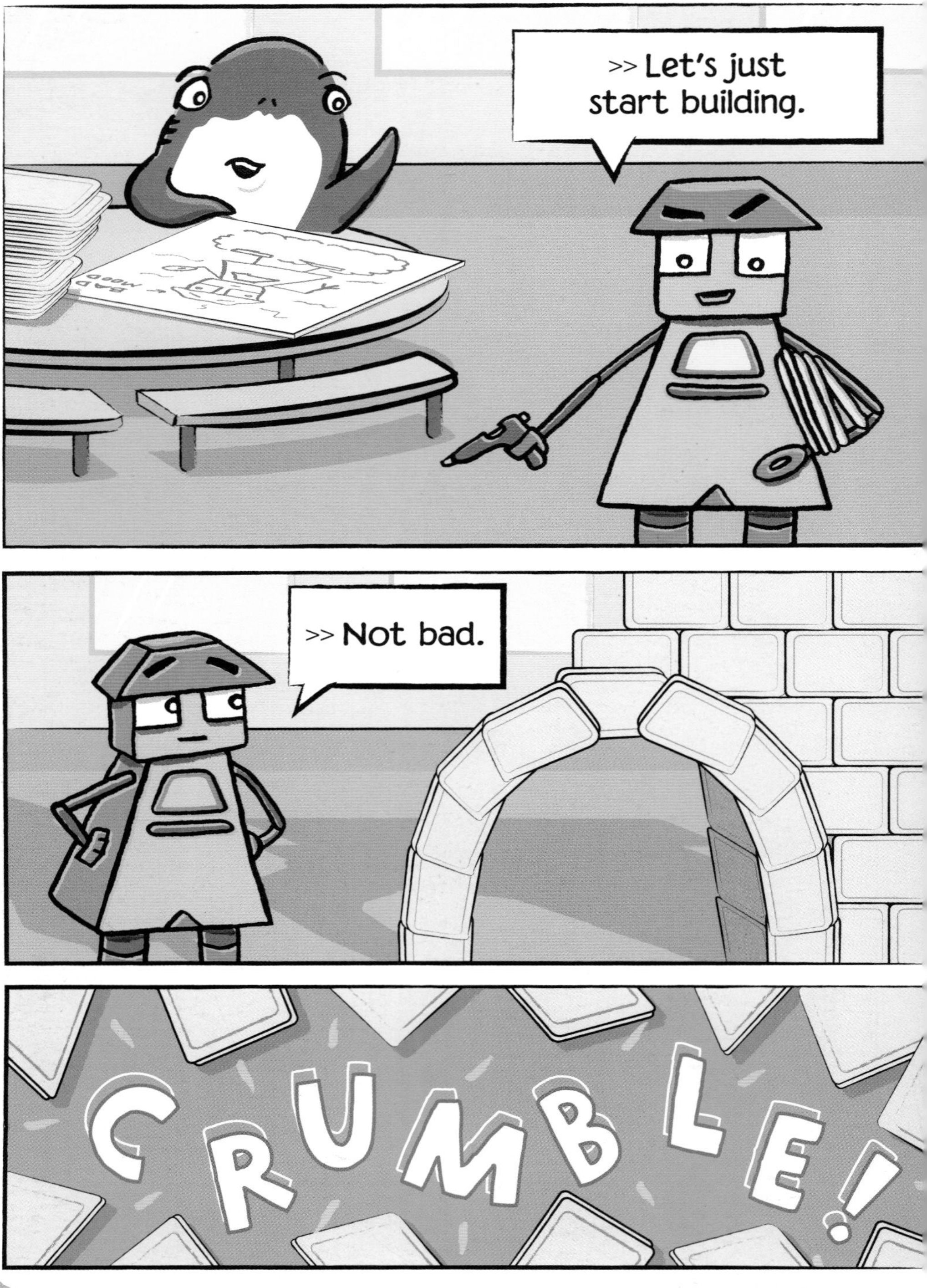
>> Let's just start building.
>> Not bad.
CRUMBLE!

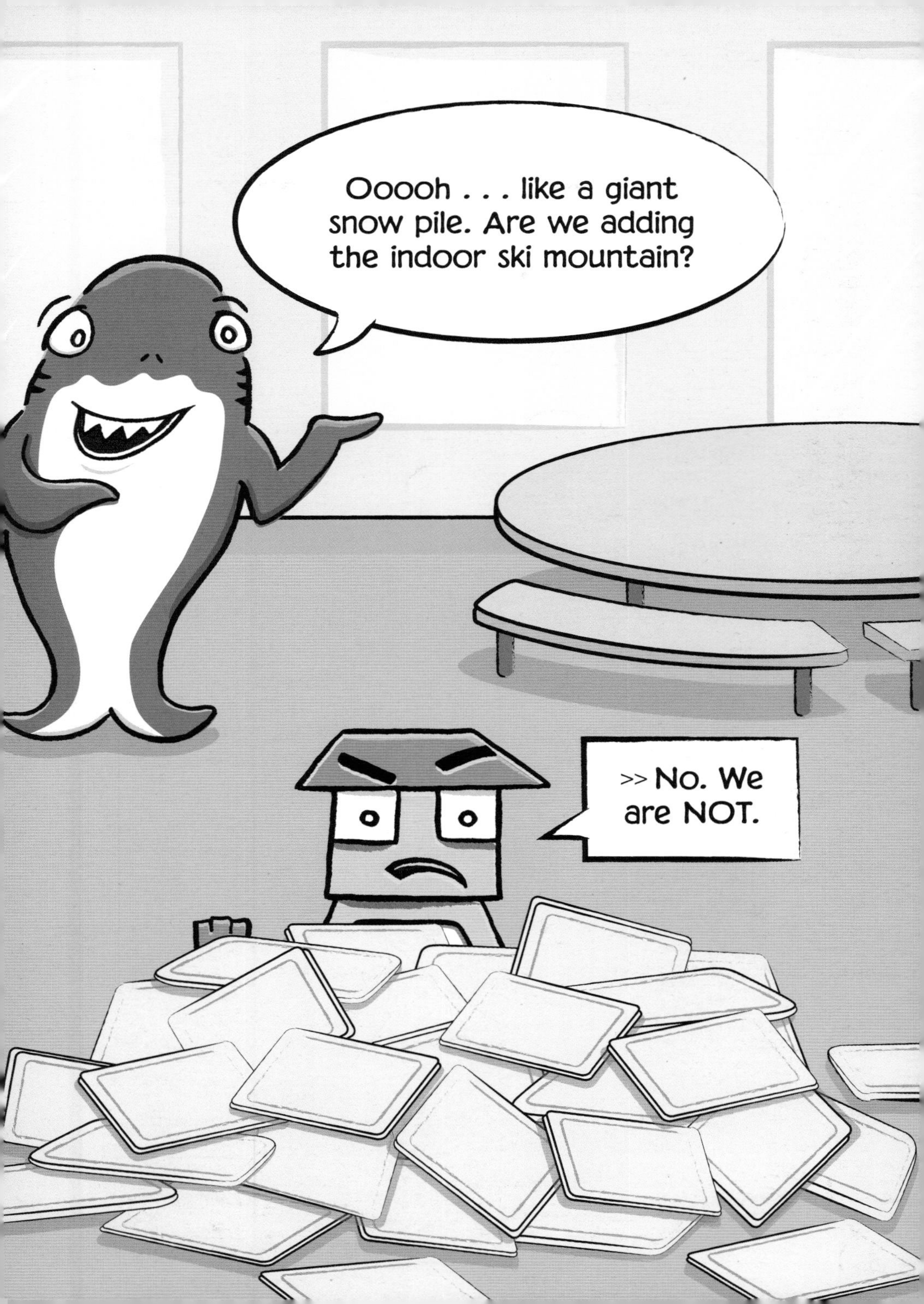
Ooooh . . . like a giant snow pile. Are we adding the indoor ski mountain?
>> No. We are NOT.

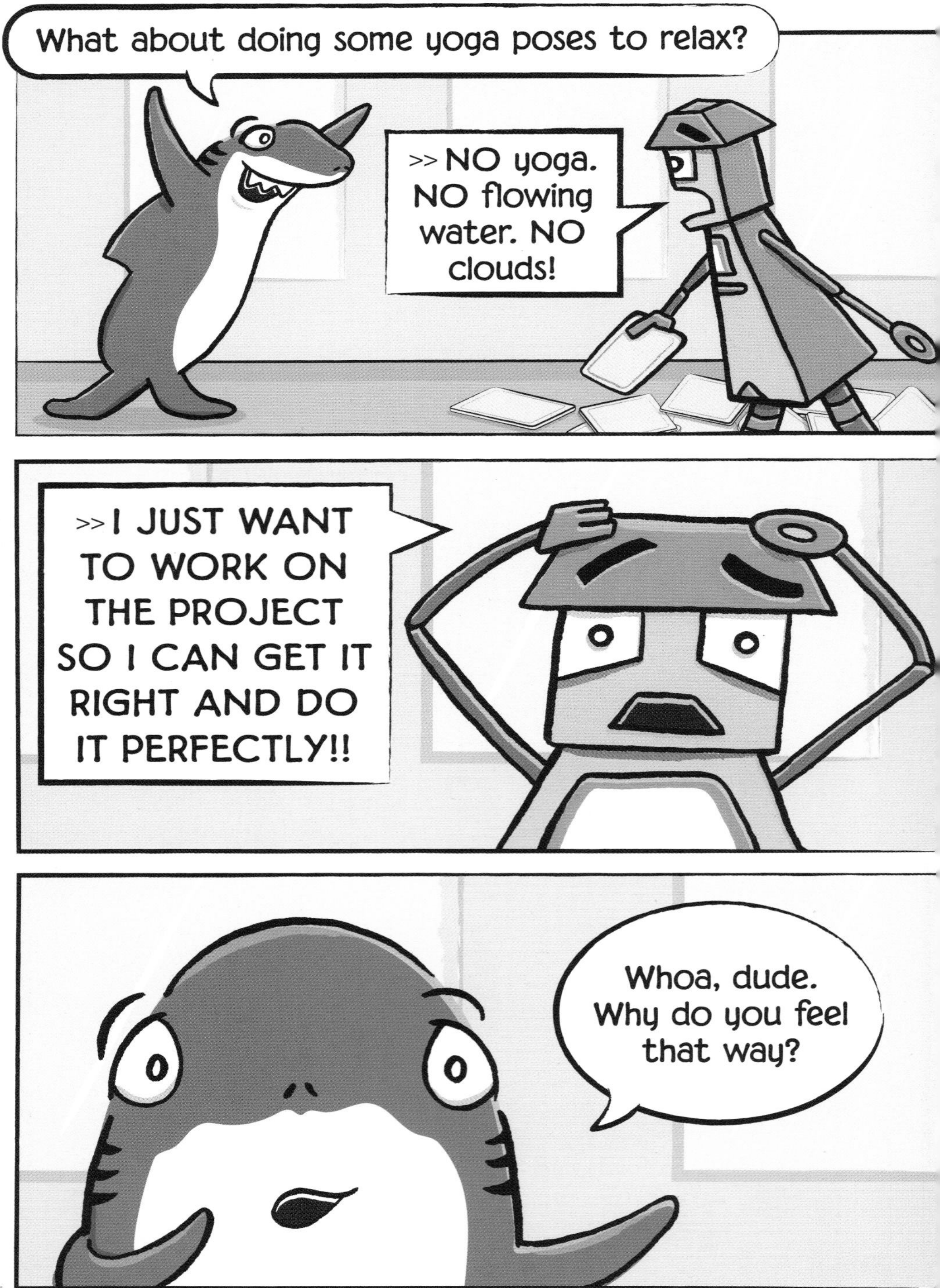
What about doing some yoga poses to relax?
>> NO yoga. NO flowing water. NO clouds!
>> I JUST WANT TO WORK ON THE PROJECT SO I CAN GET IT RIGHT AND DO IT PERFECTLY!!
Whoa, dude. Why do you feel that way?

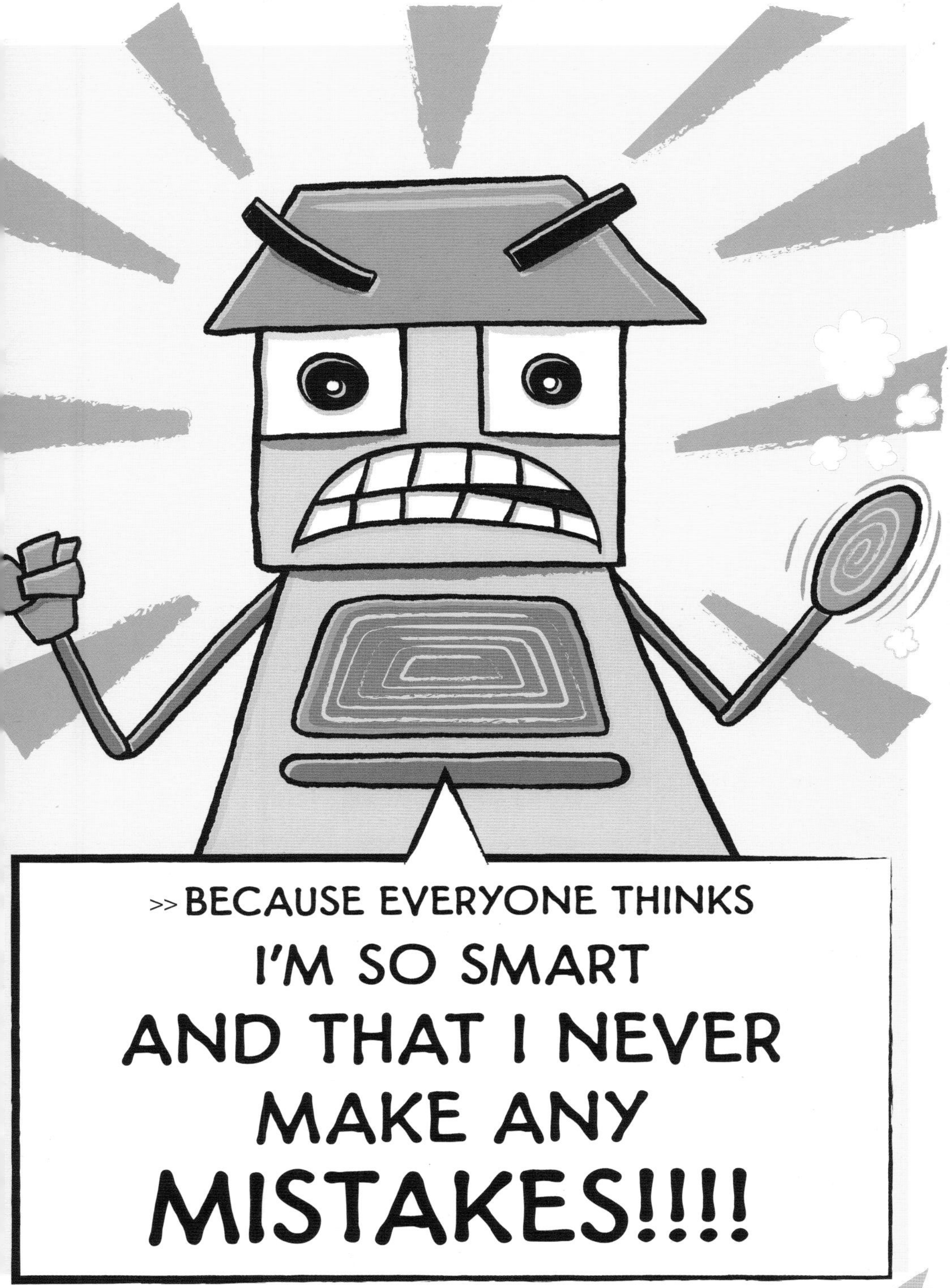
>> BECAUSE EVERYONE THINKS
I'M SO SMART
AND THAT I NEVER
MAKE ANY
MISTAKES!!!!

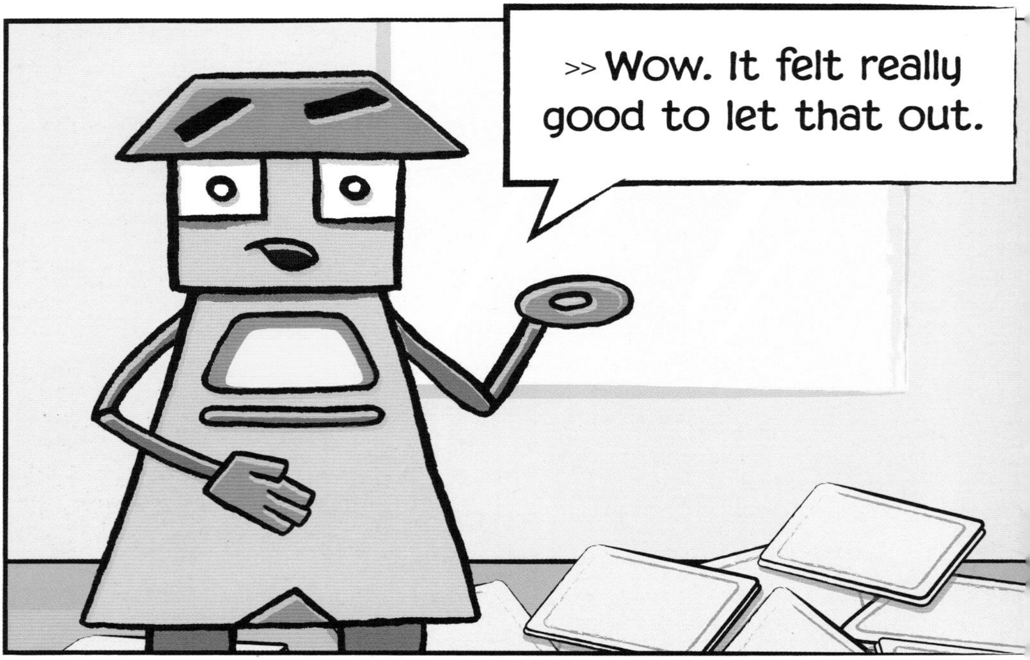
>> Wow. It felt really good to let that out.

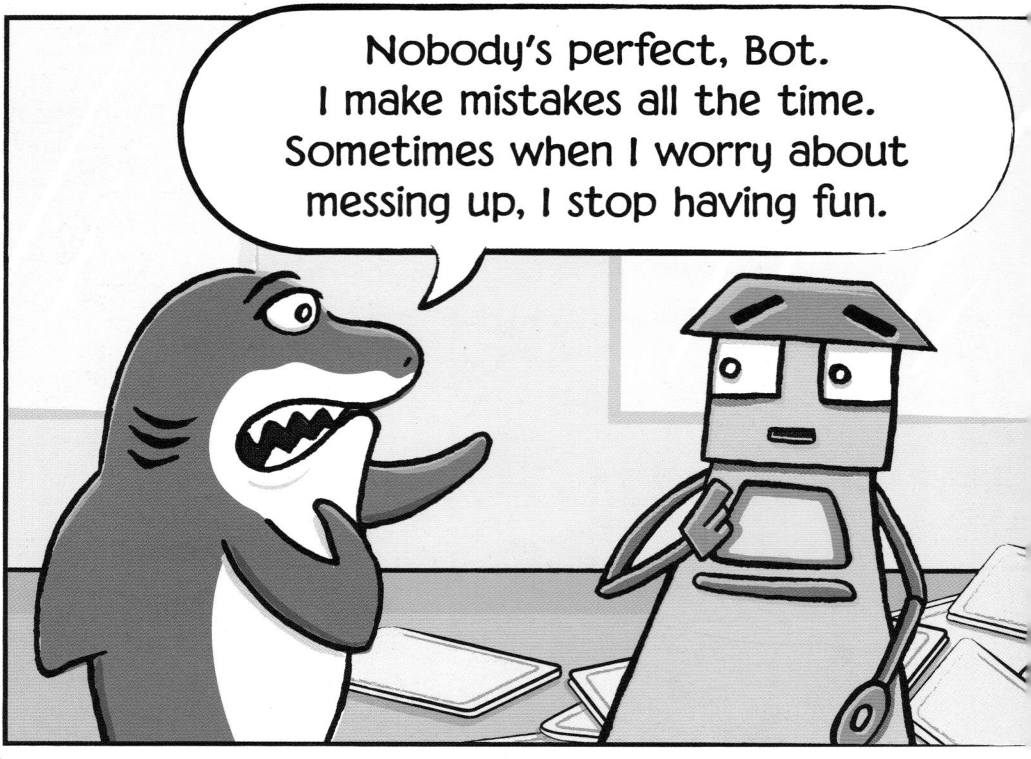
Nobody's perfect, Bot. I make mistakes all the time. Sometimes when I worry about messing up, I stop having fun.

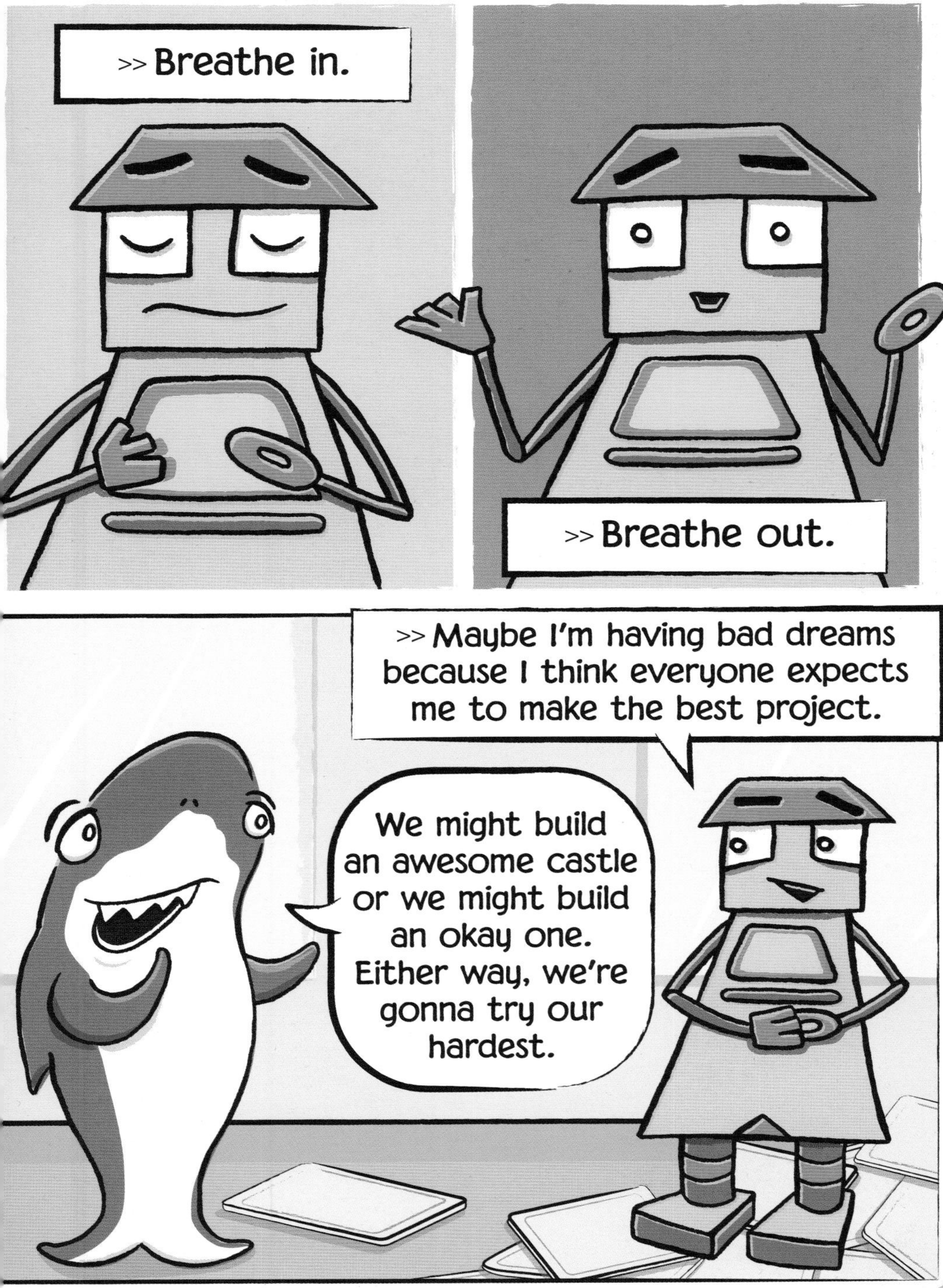
>> Breathe in.
>> Breathe out.
>> Maybe I'm having bad dreams because I think everyone expects me to make the best project.
We might build an awesome castle or we might build an okay one. Either way, we're gonna try our hardest.

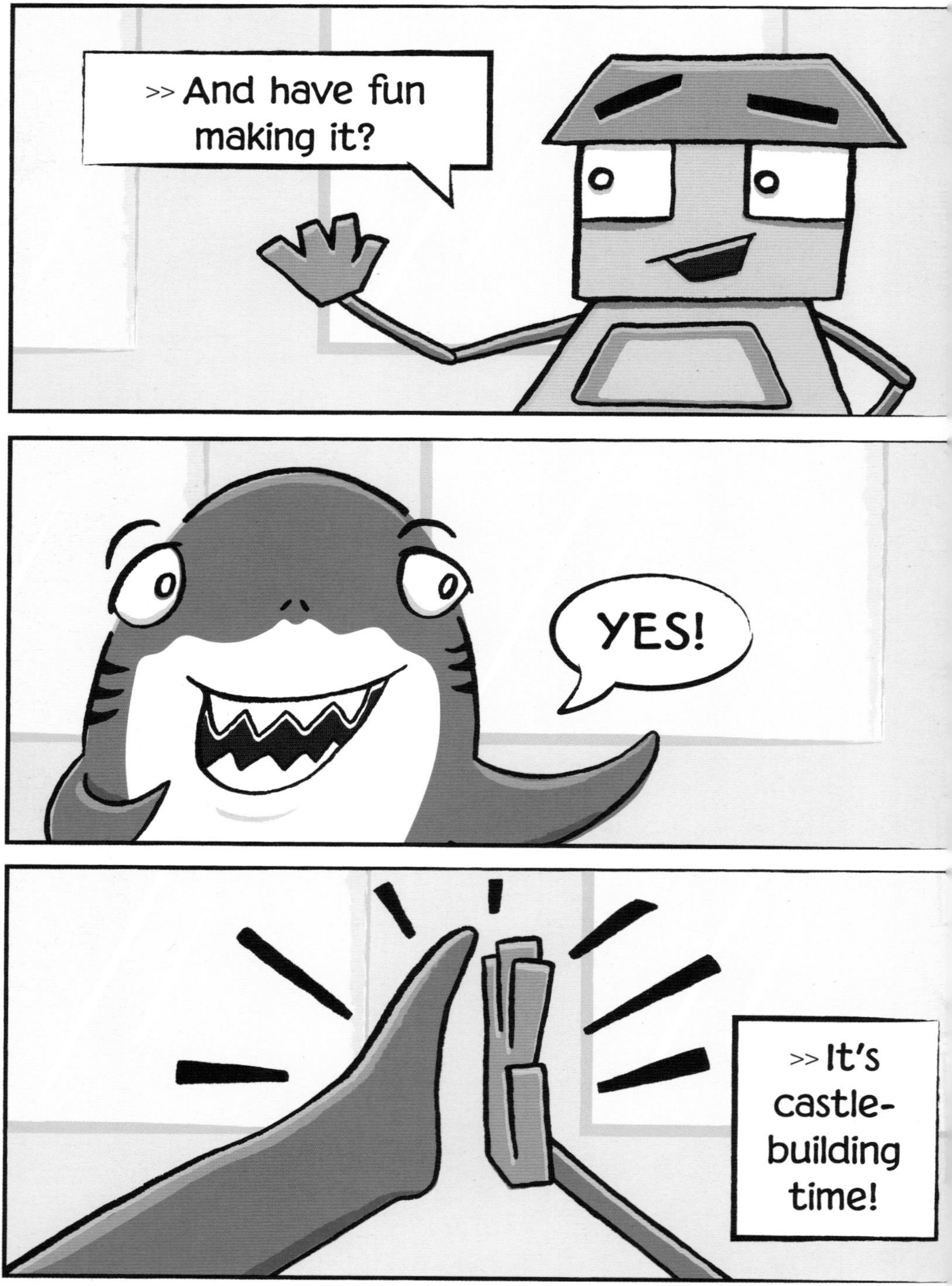
>> And have fun making it?
YES!
>> It's castle-building time!

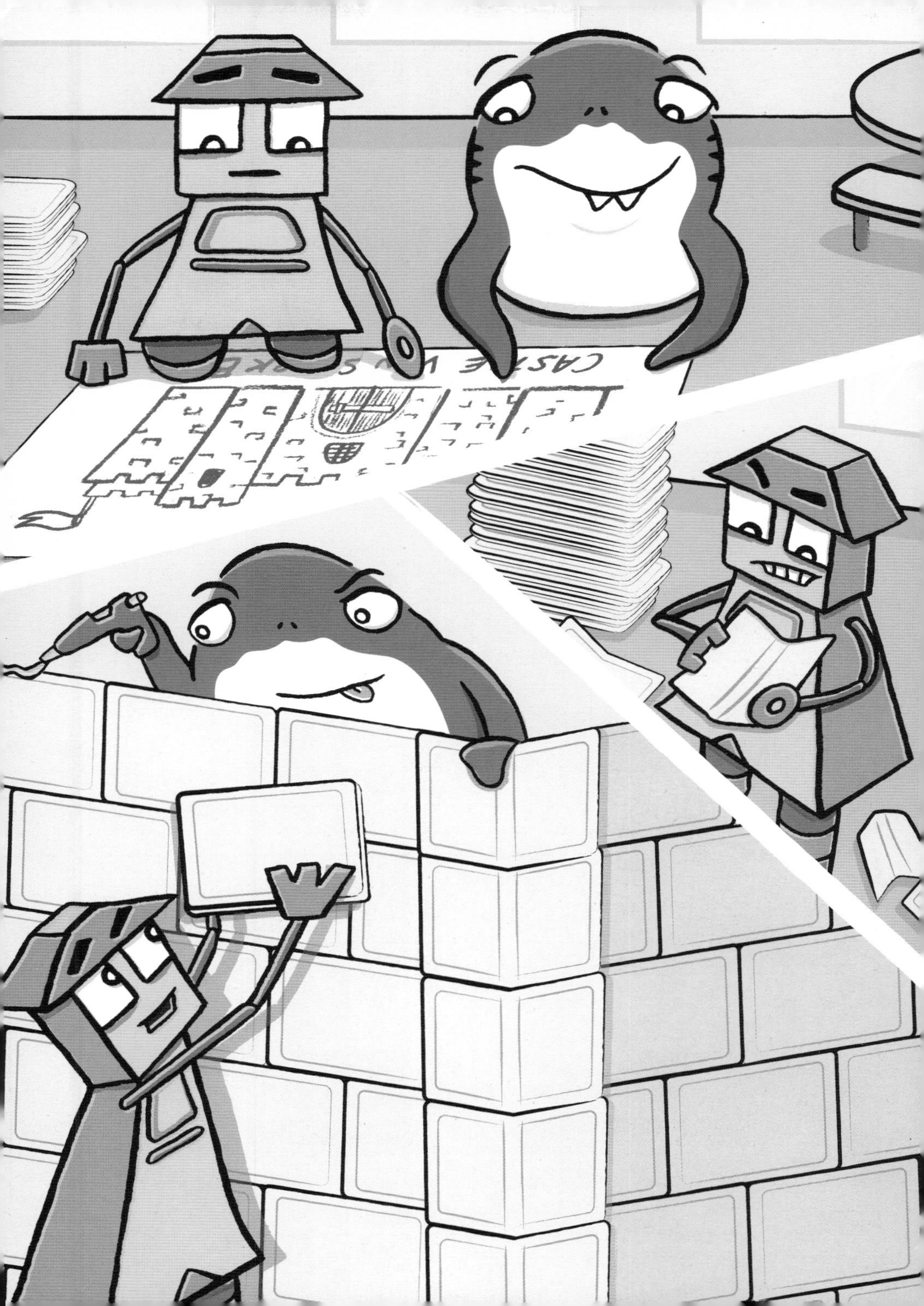

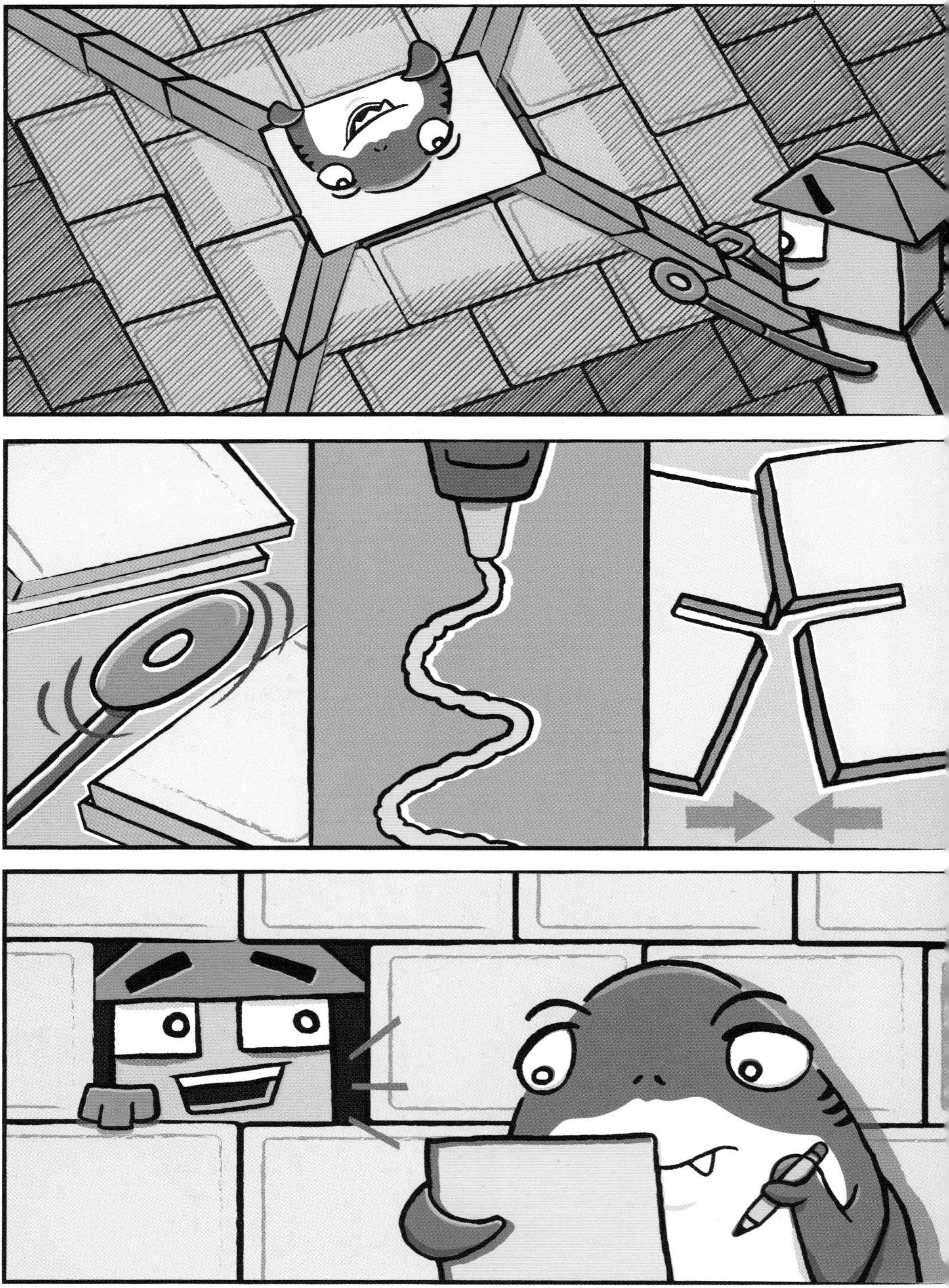

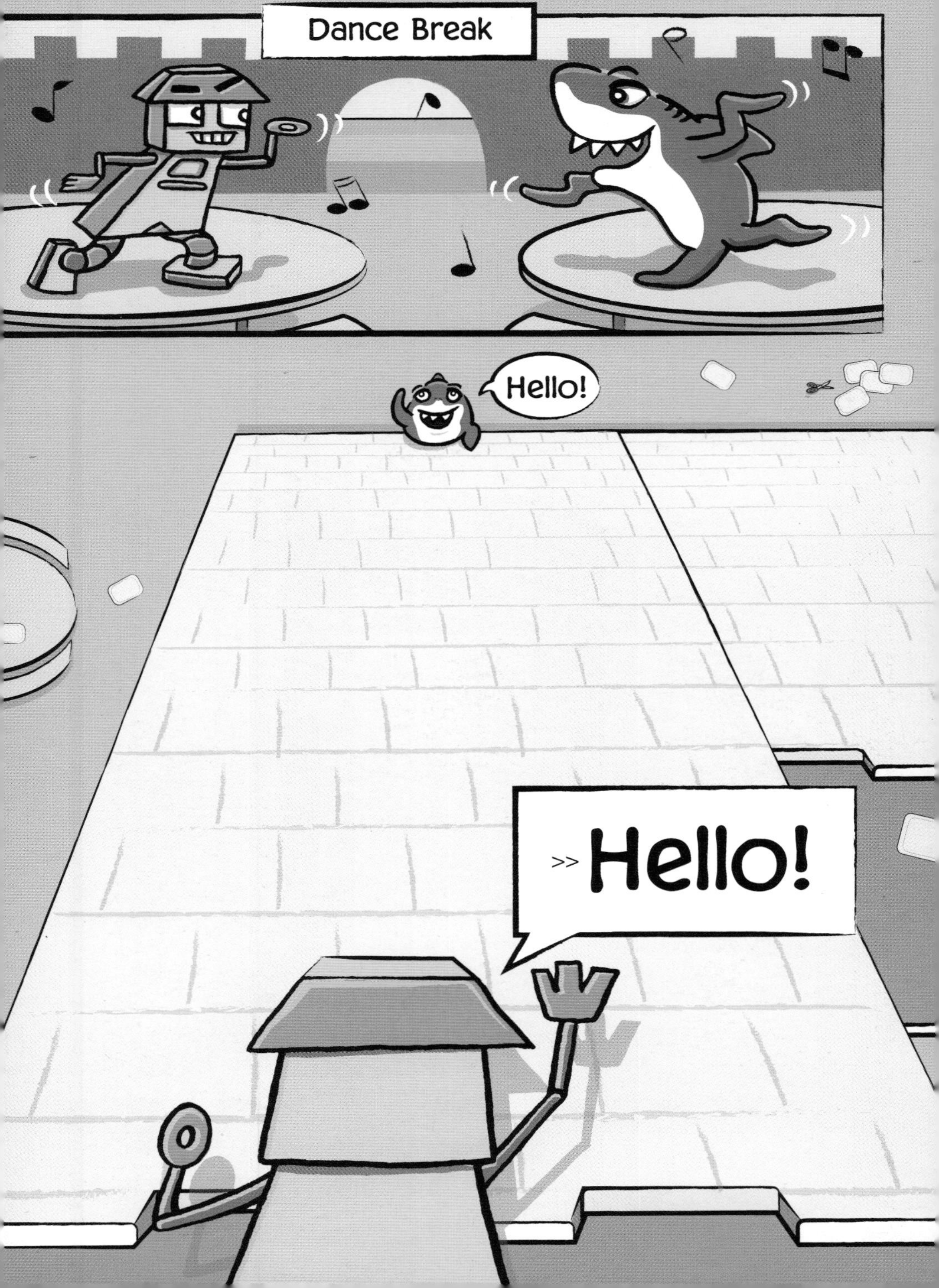
Dance Break
Hello!
>>Hello!

Chapter 7

Lunchroom Lockdown

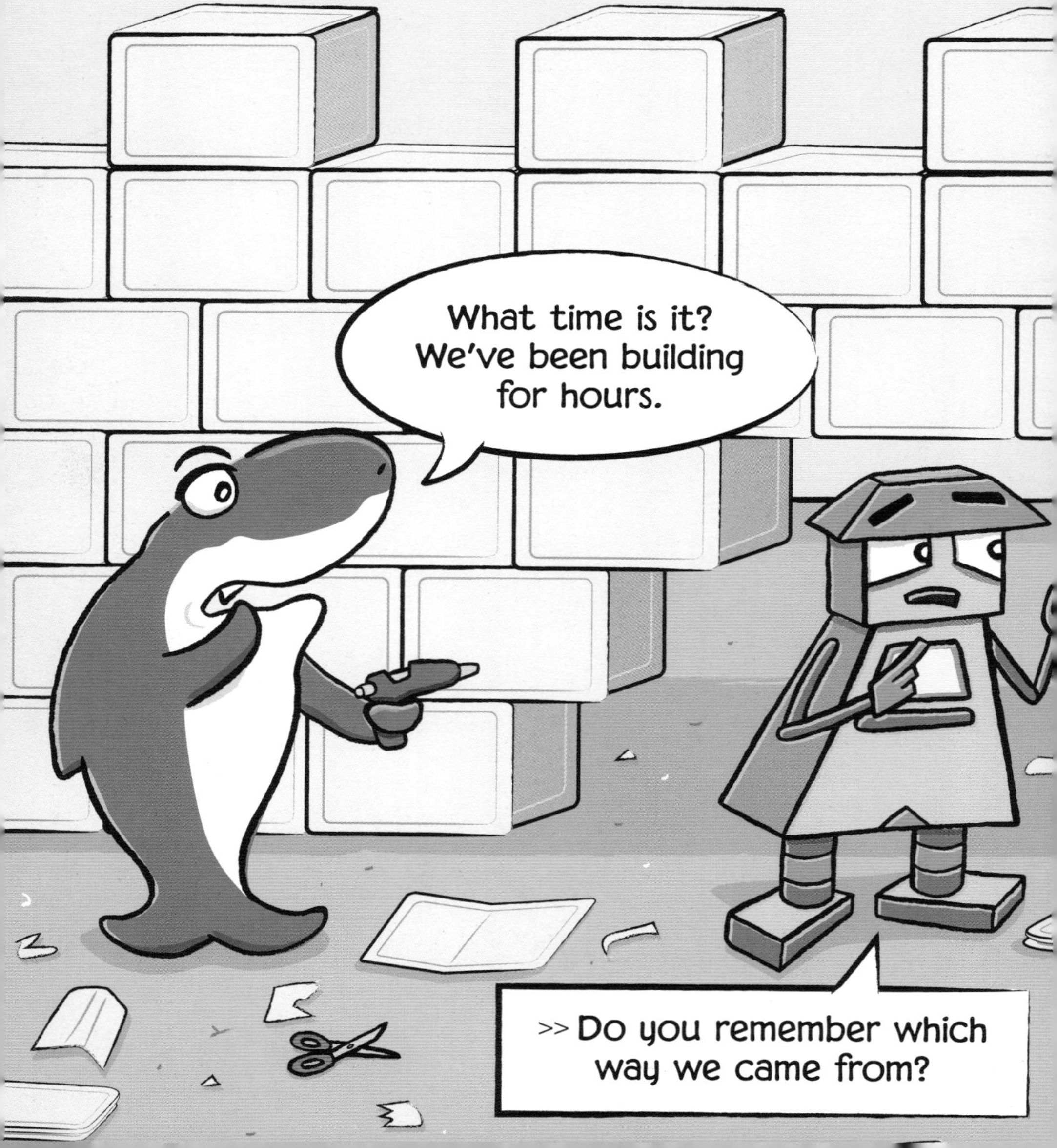
What time is it? We've been building for hours.
>> Do you remember which way we came from?

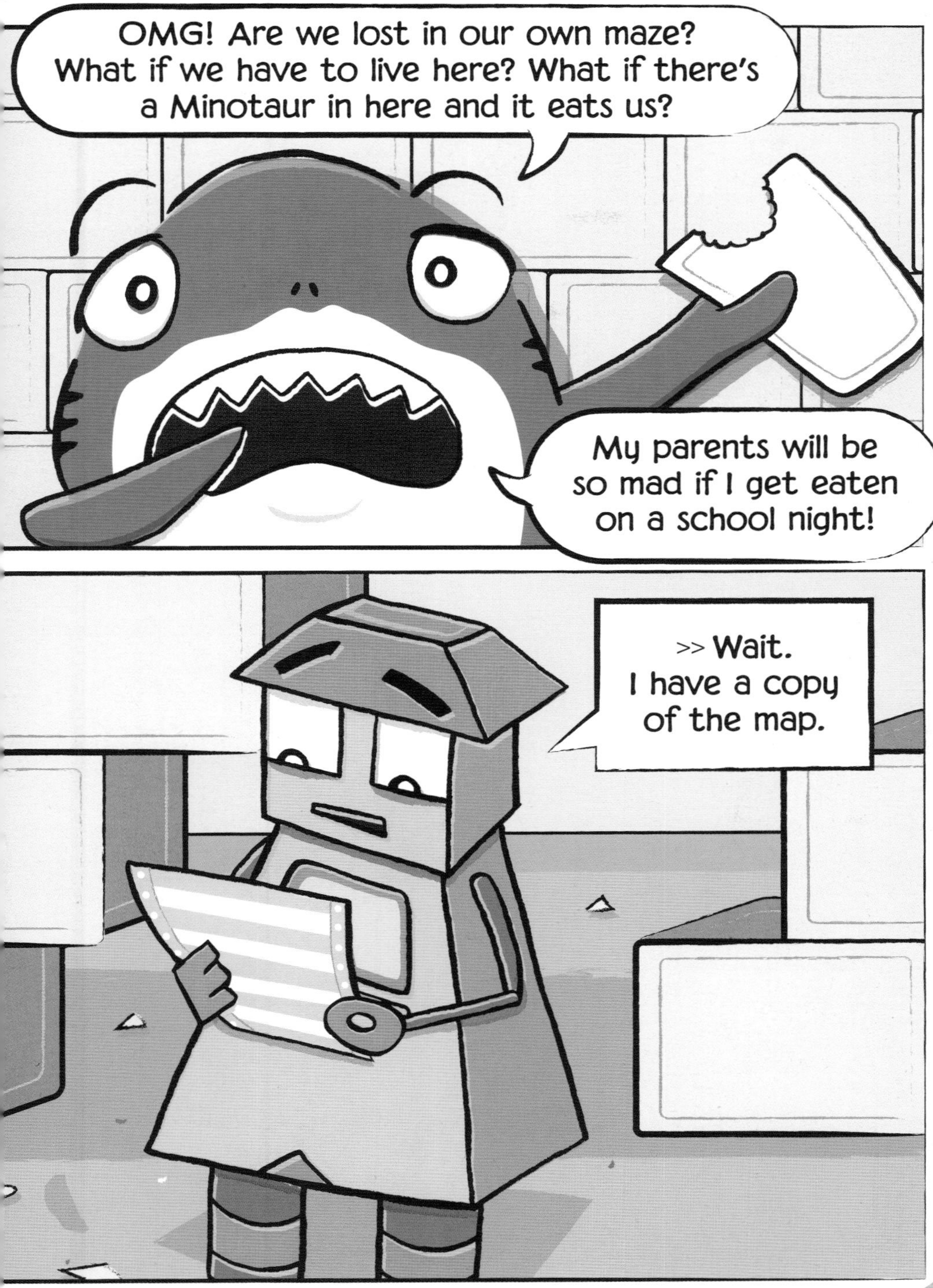
OMG! Are we lost in our own maze? What if we have to live here? What if there's a Minotaur in here and it eats us?
My parents will be so mad if I get eaten on a school night!
>> Wait. I have a copy of the map.

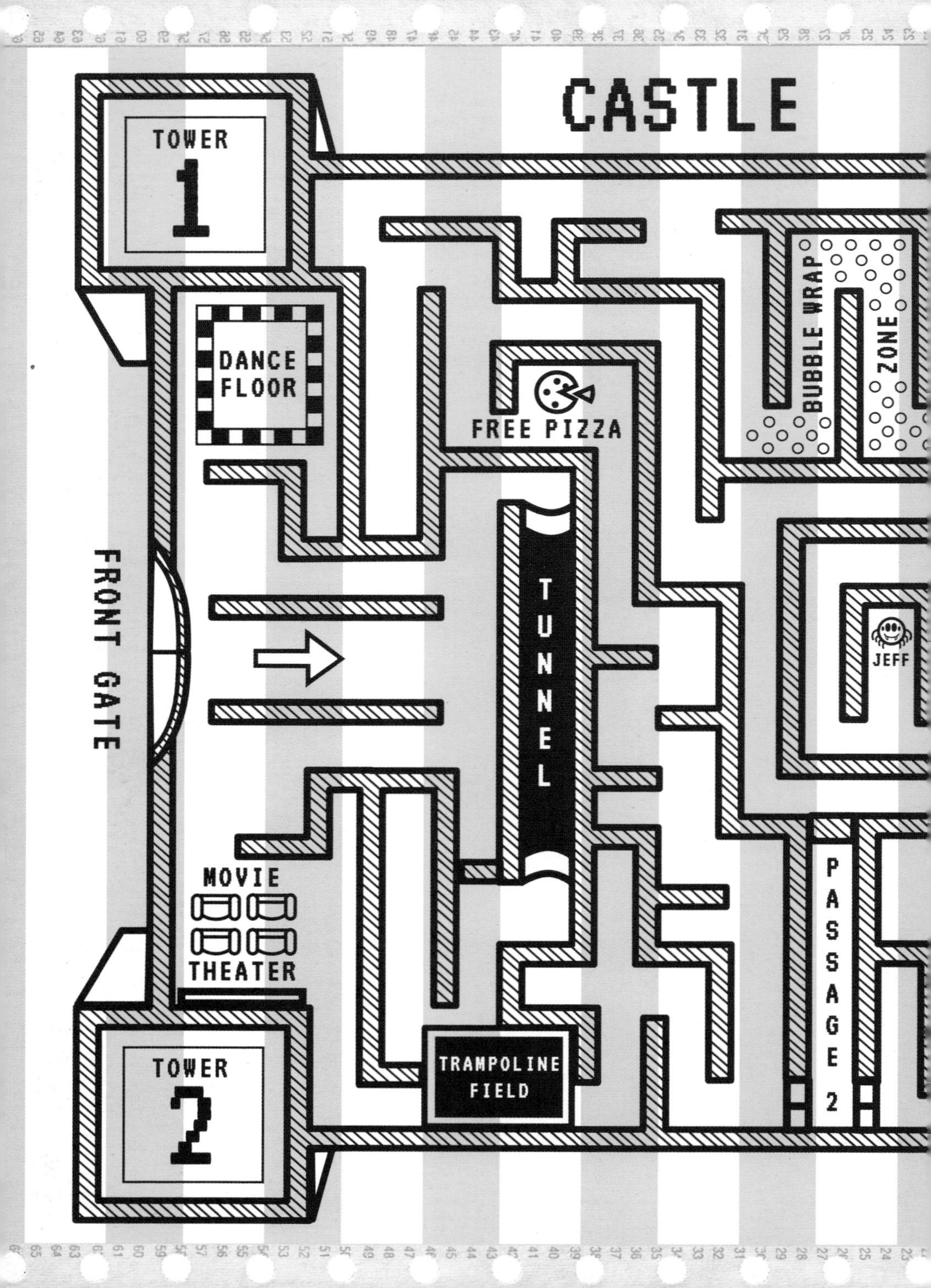
CASTLE
TOWER 1
DANCE FLOOR
FREE PIZZA
BUBBLE WRAP ZONE
FRONT GATE
TUNNEL
JEFF
MOVIE THEATER
TOWER 2
TRAMPOLINE FIELD
PASSAGE 2

MAP

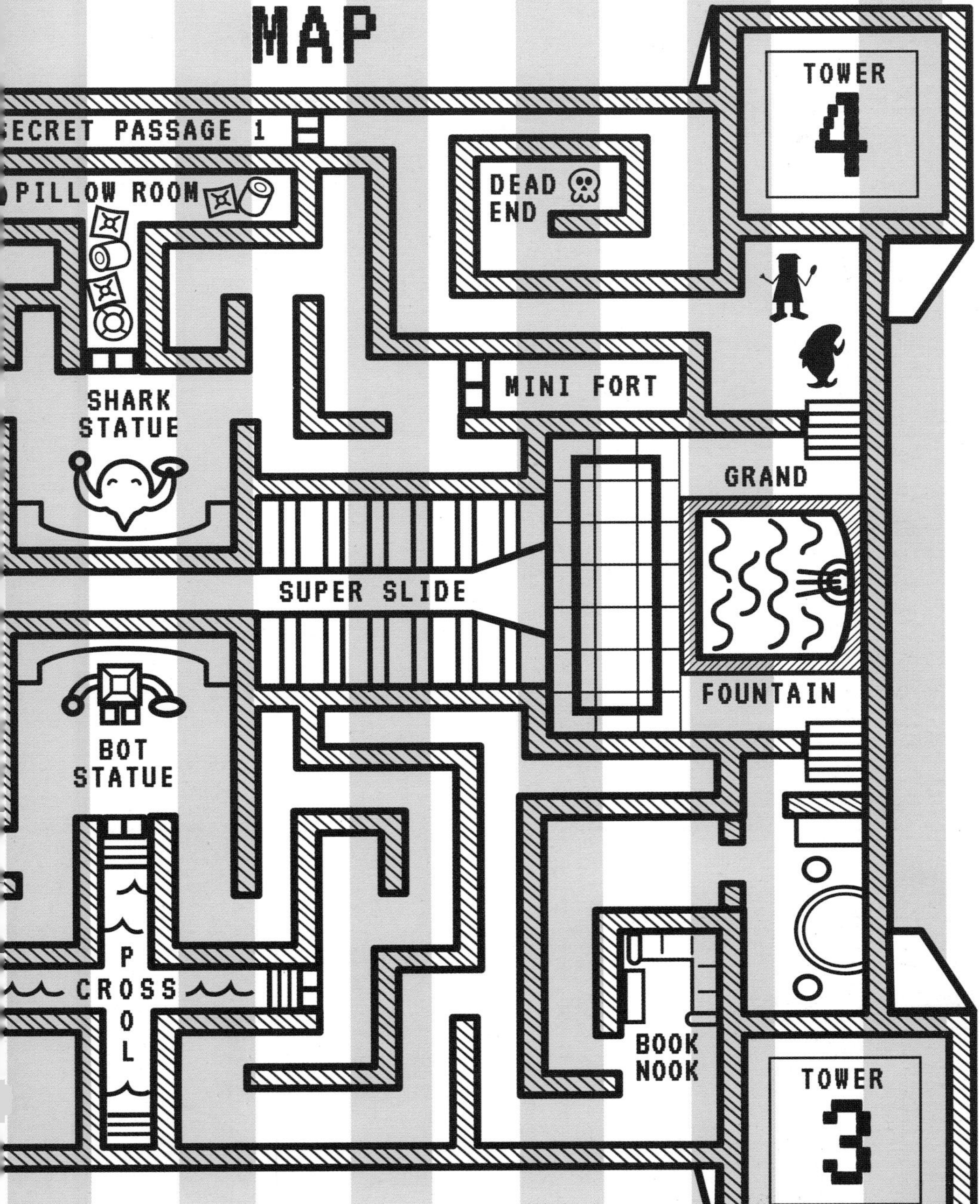

TOWER 4
SECRET PASSAGE 1
DEAD END
PILLOW ROOM
MINI FORT
SHARK STATUE
GRAND FOUNTAIN
SUPER SLIDE
BOT STATUE
CROSS POOL
BOOK NOOK
TOWER 3

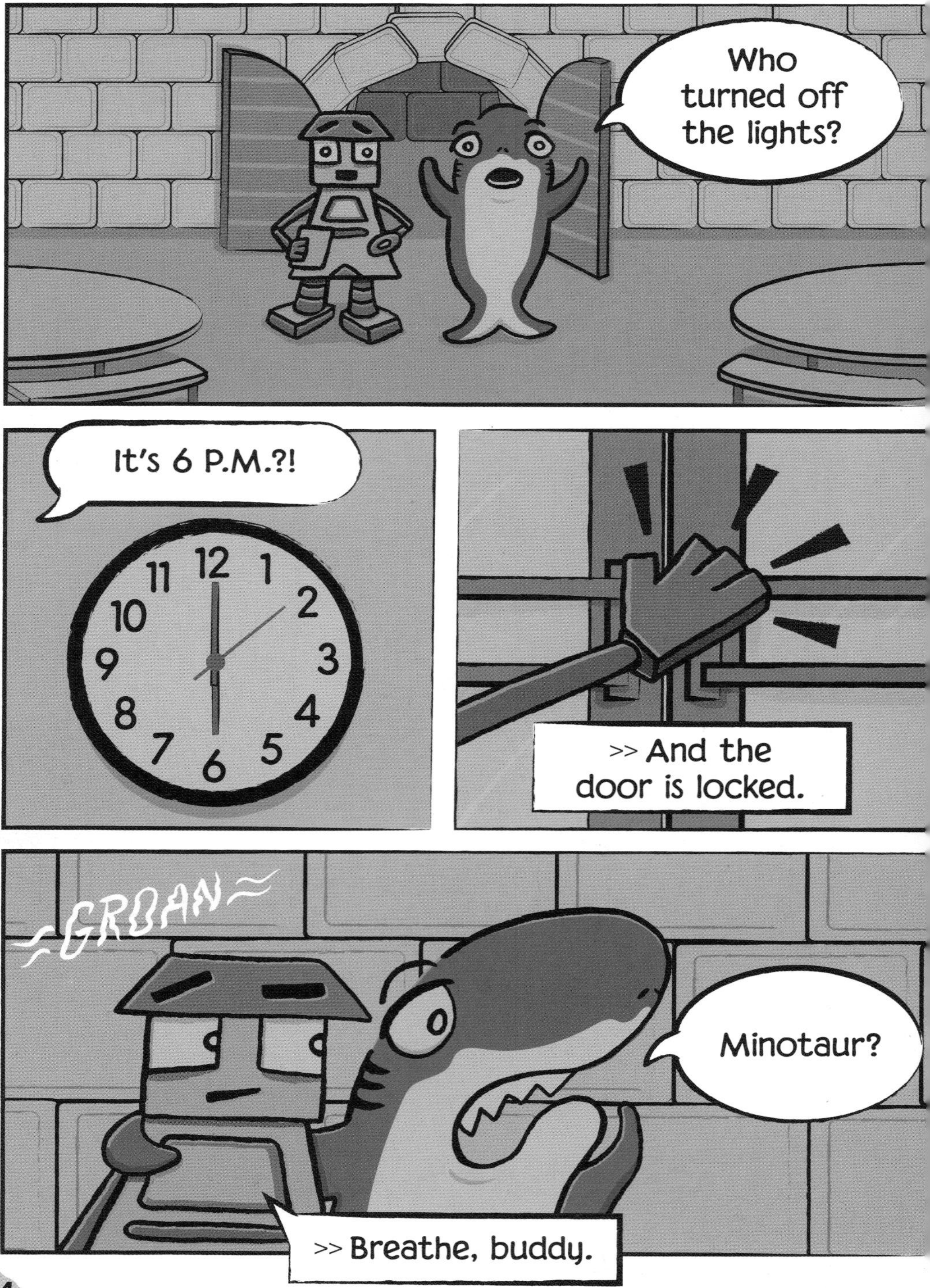
Who turned off the lights?
It's 6 P.M.?!
12
1
2
3
4
5
6
7
8
9
10
11
>> And the door is locked.
GROAN
Minotaur?
>> Breathe, buddy.

Chapter 8

Zo-Nuts! Glo-Nuts?

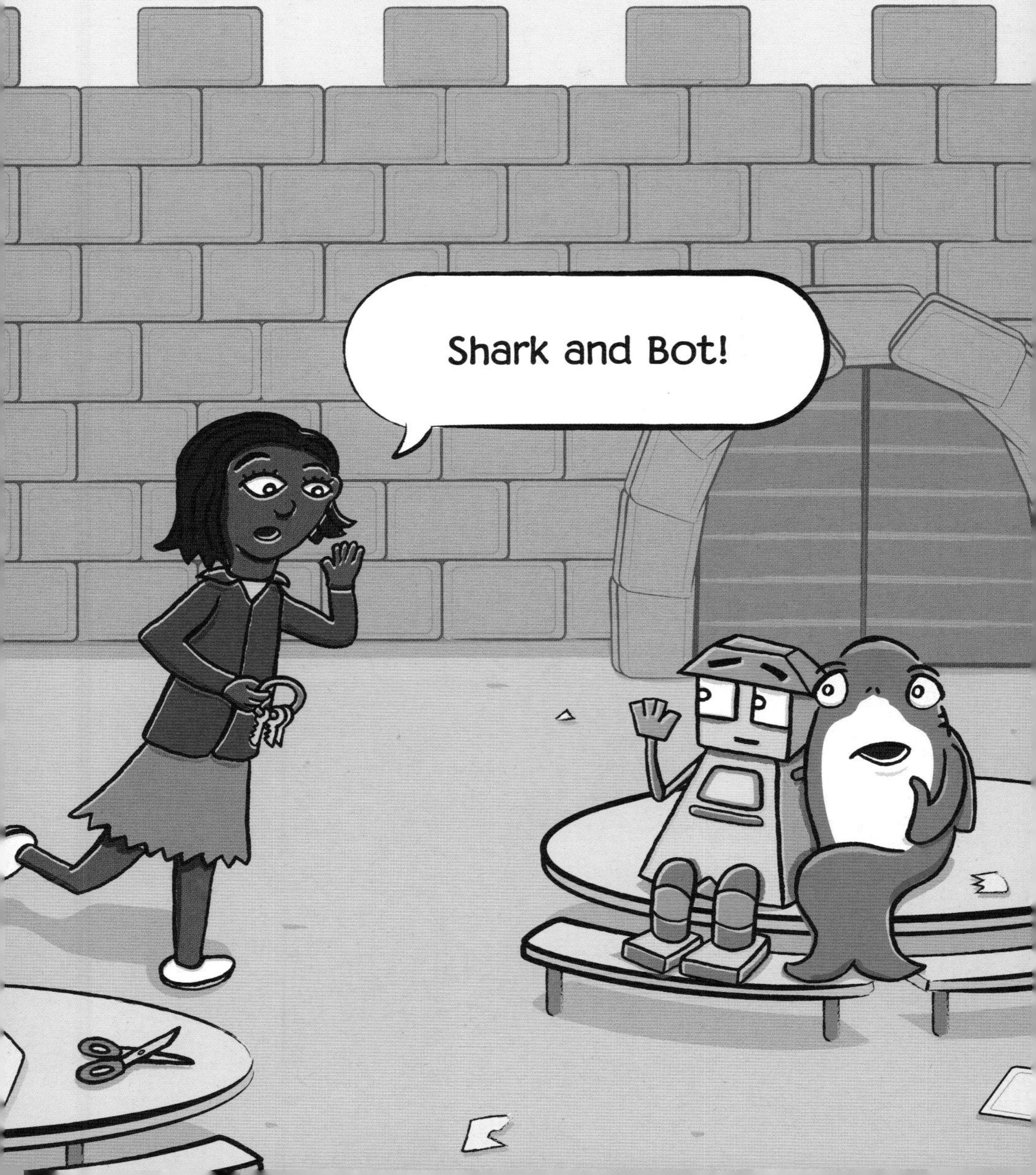
Shark and Bot!

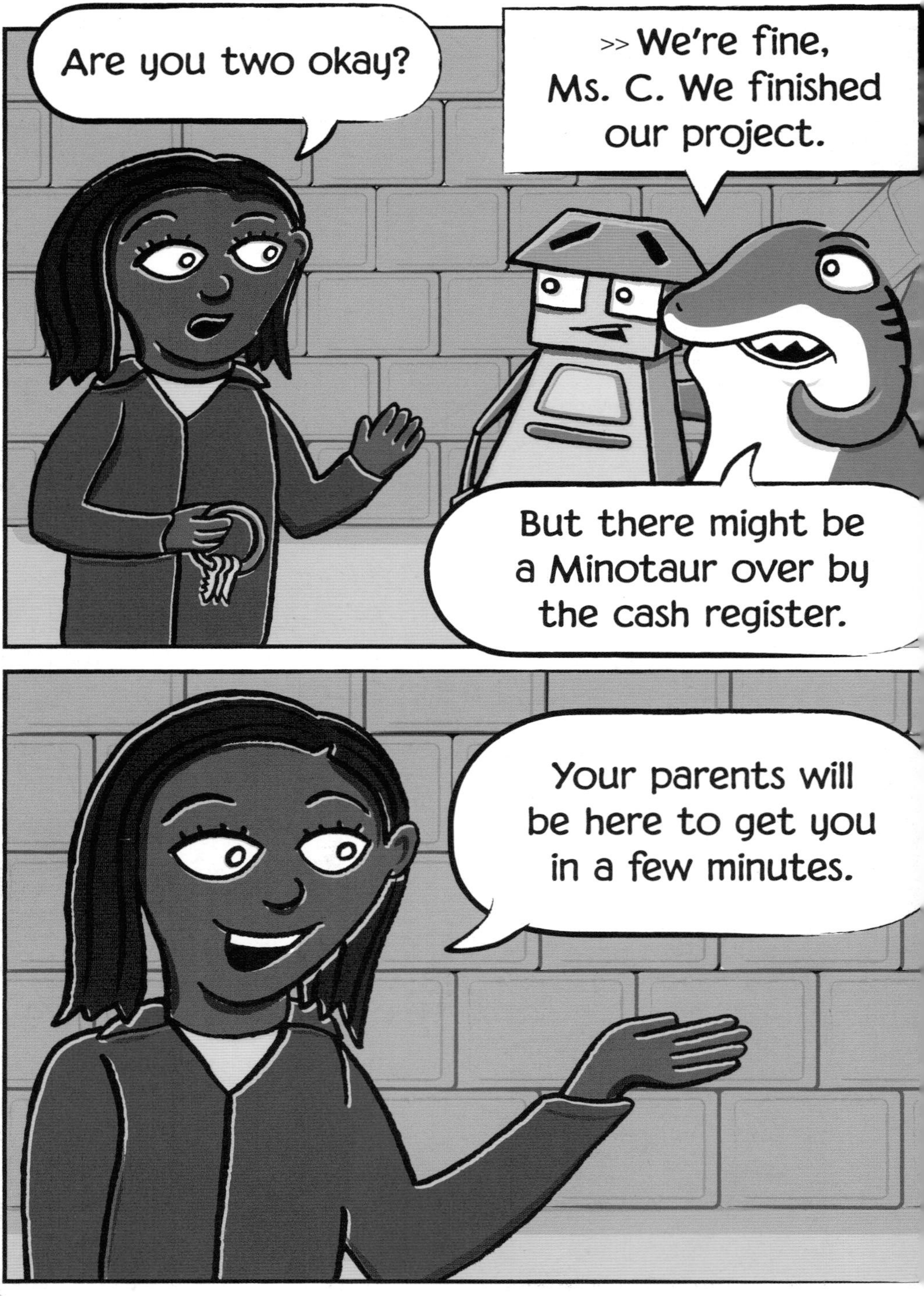
Are you two okay?
>> We're fine, Ms. C. We finished our project.
But there might be a Minotaur over by the cash register.
Your parents will be here to get you in a few minutes.

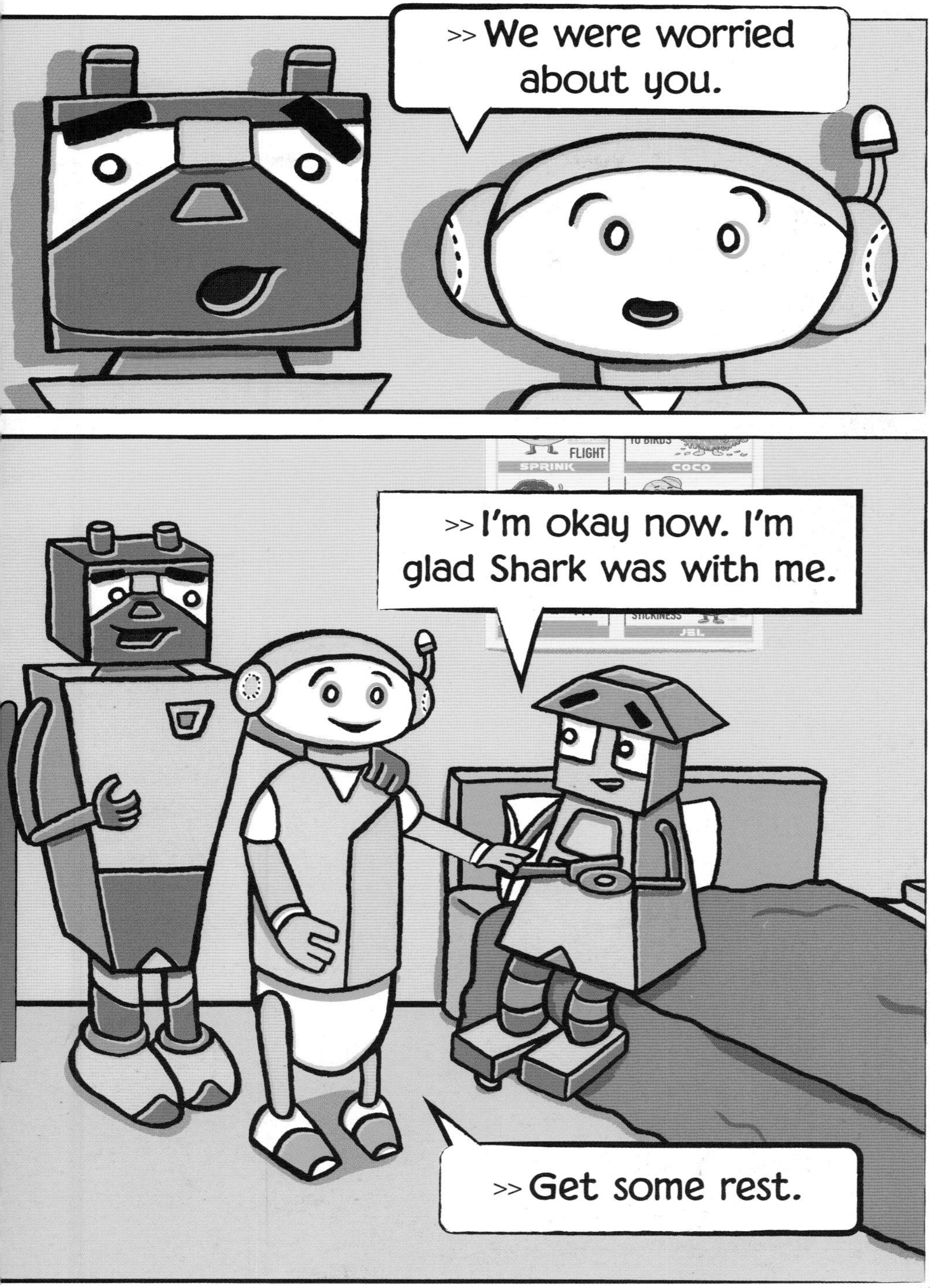
>> We were worried about you.
FLIGHT
SPRINK
COCO
JEL
>> I'm okay now. I'm glad Shark was with me.
>> Get some rest.

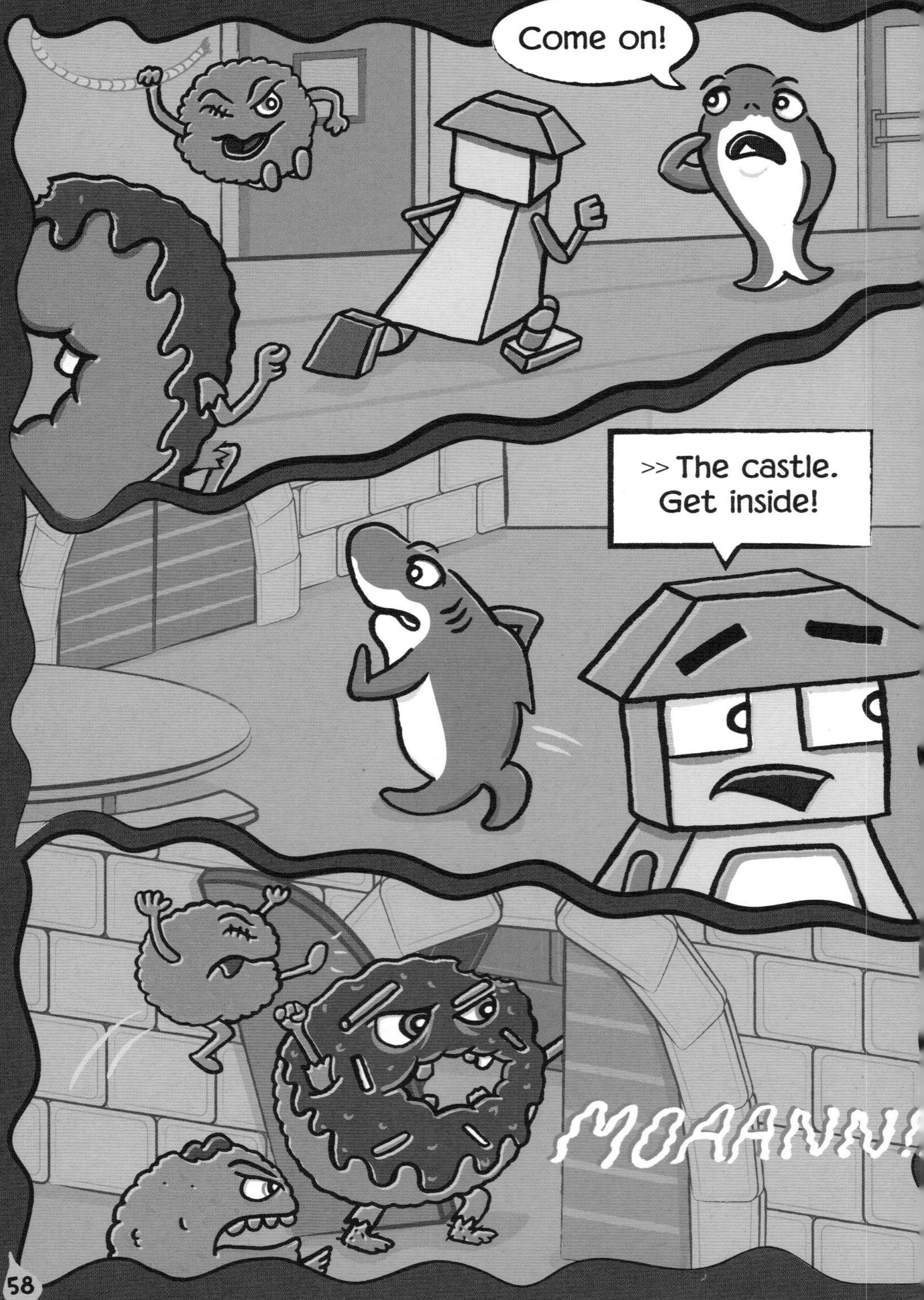
Come on!
>> The castle. Get inside!
MOAANN!

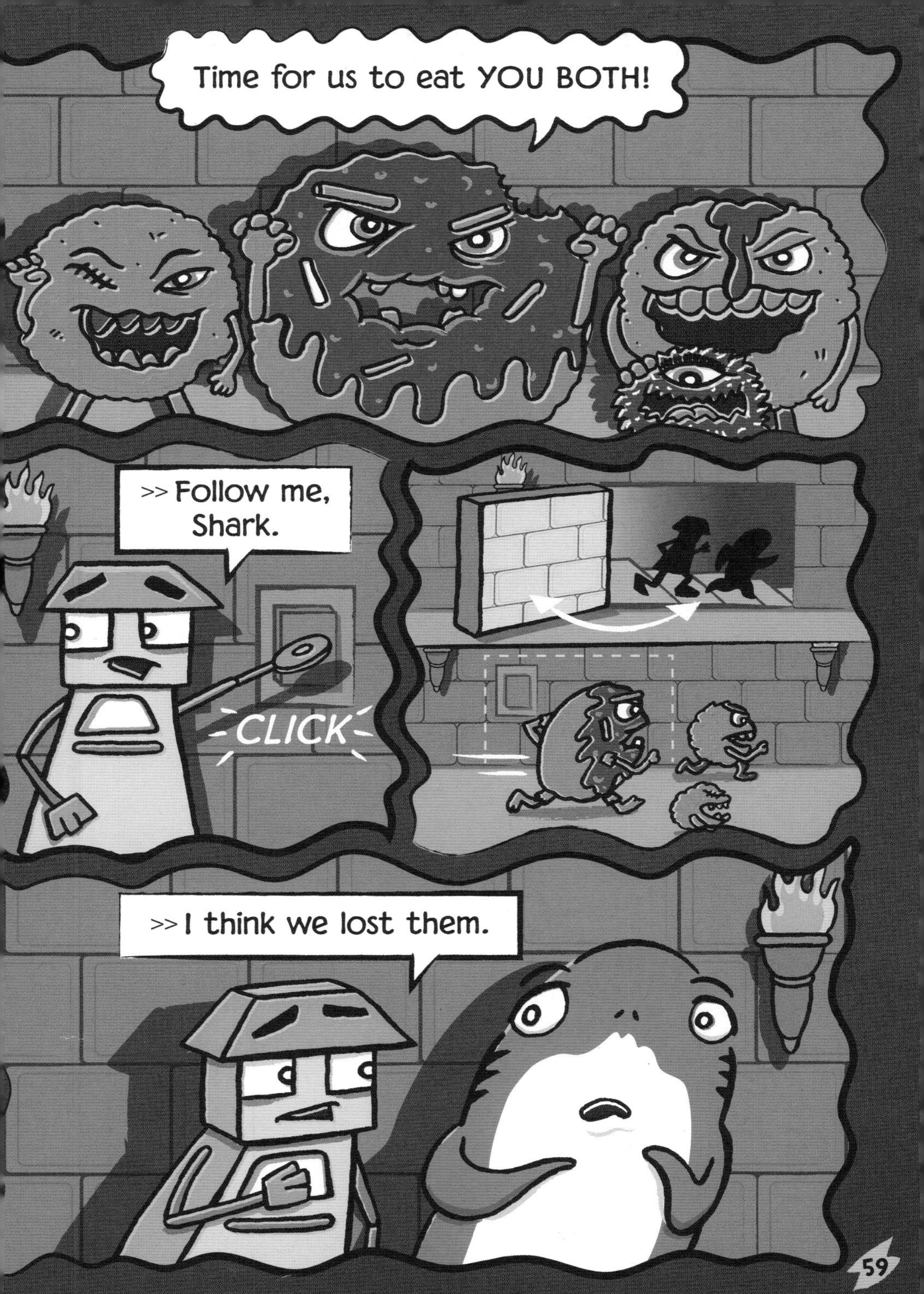
Time for us to eat YOU BOTH!
>> Follow me, Shark.
CLICK
>> I think we lost them.

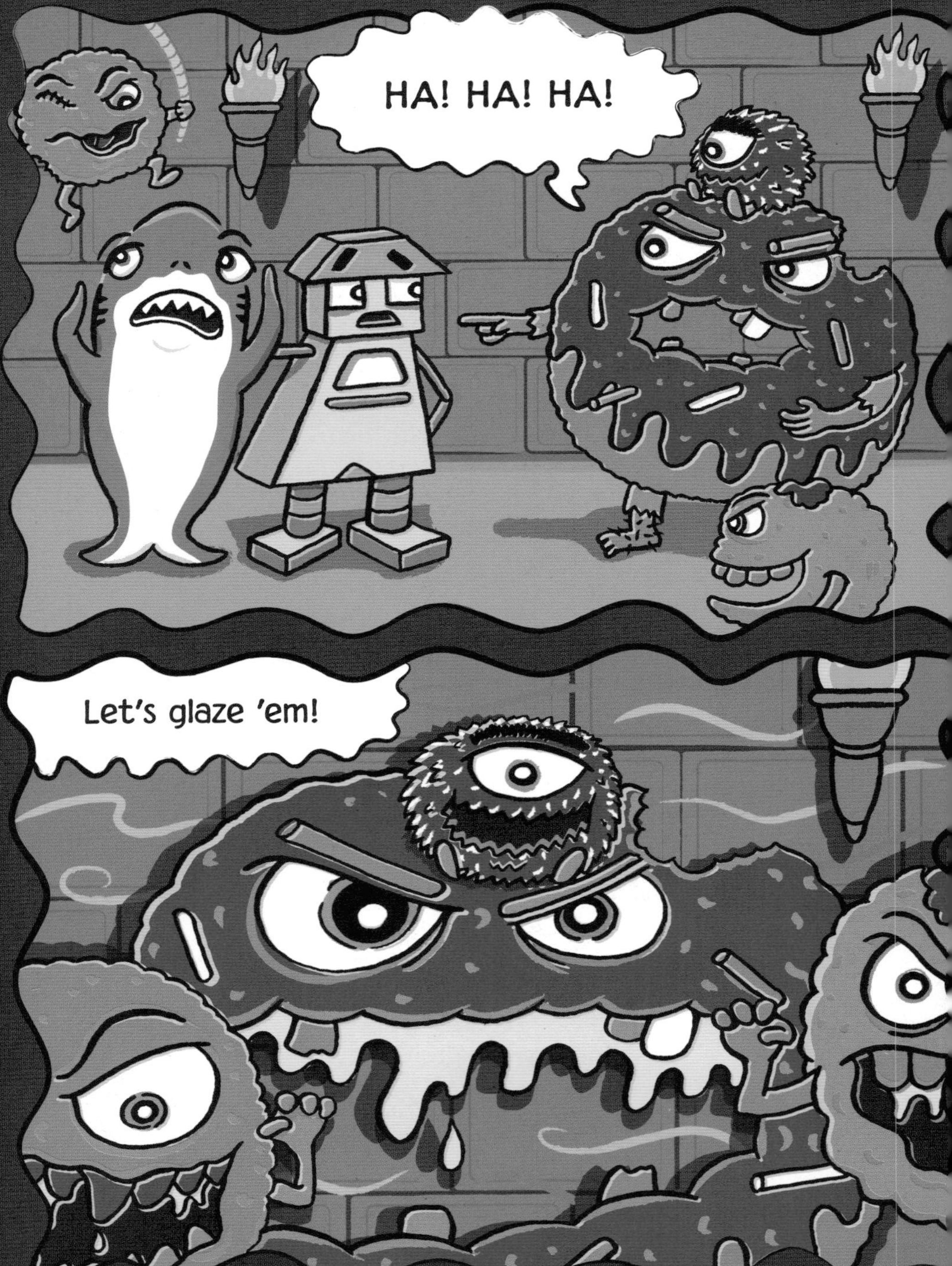
HA! HA! HA!
Let's glaze 'em!

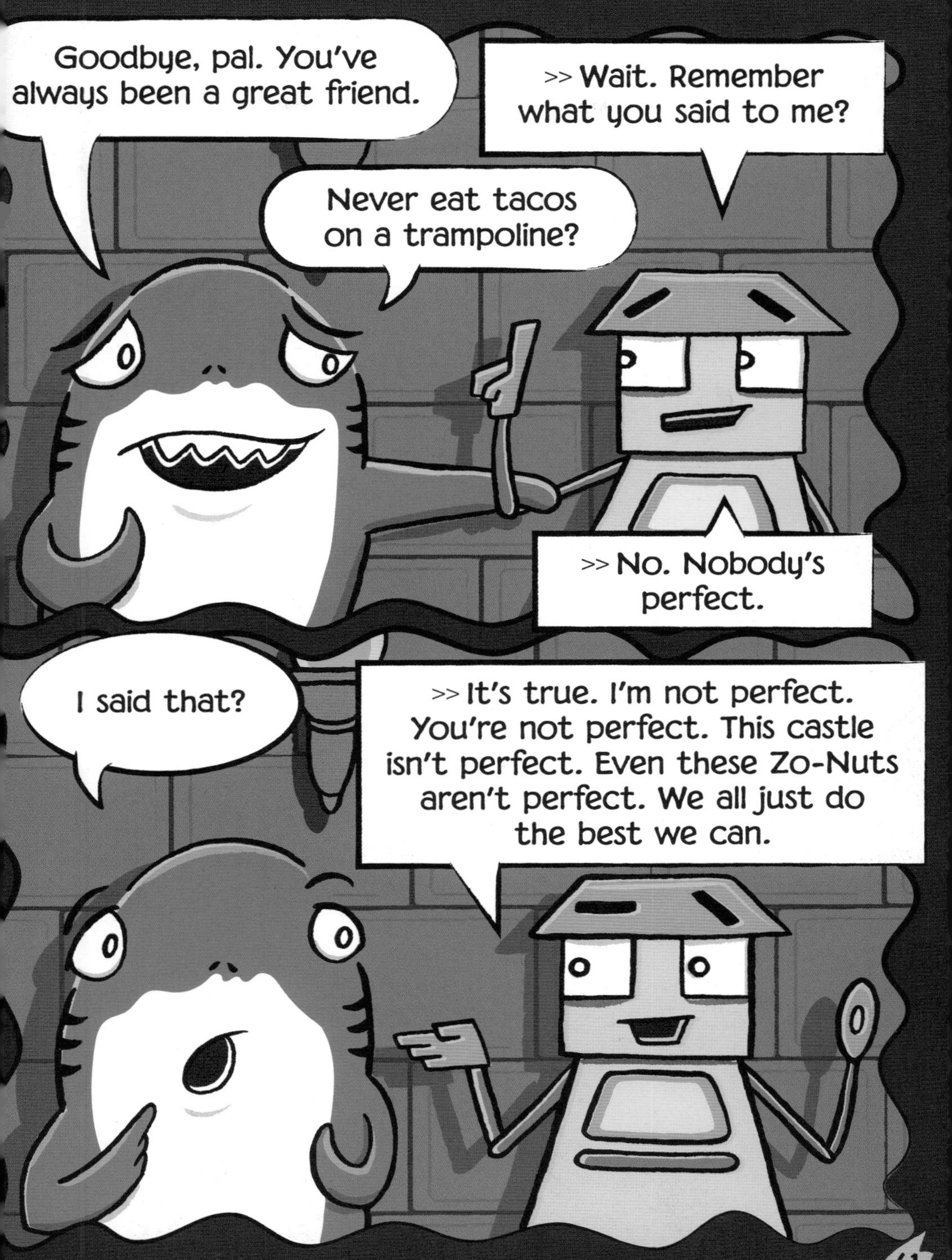
Goodbye, pal. You've always been a great friend.
>> Wait. Remember what you said to me?
Never eat tacos on a trampoline?
>> No. Nobody's perfect.
I said that?
>> It's true. I'm not perfect. You're not perfect. This castle isn't perfect. Even these Zo-Nuts aren't perfect. We all just do the best we can.

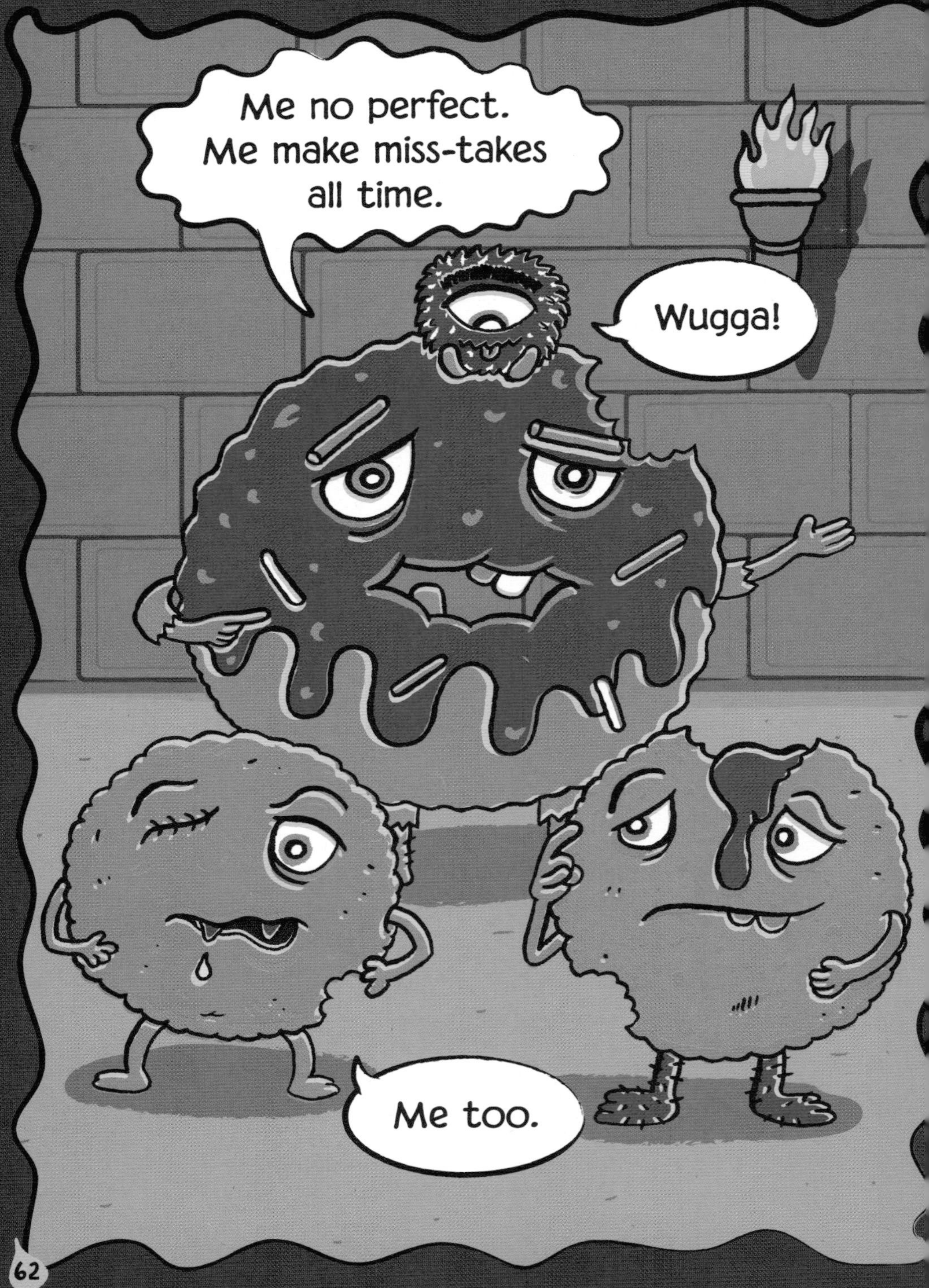
Me no perfect. Me make miss-takes all time.
Wugga!
Me too.

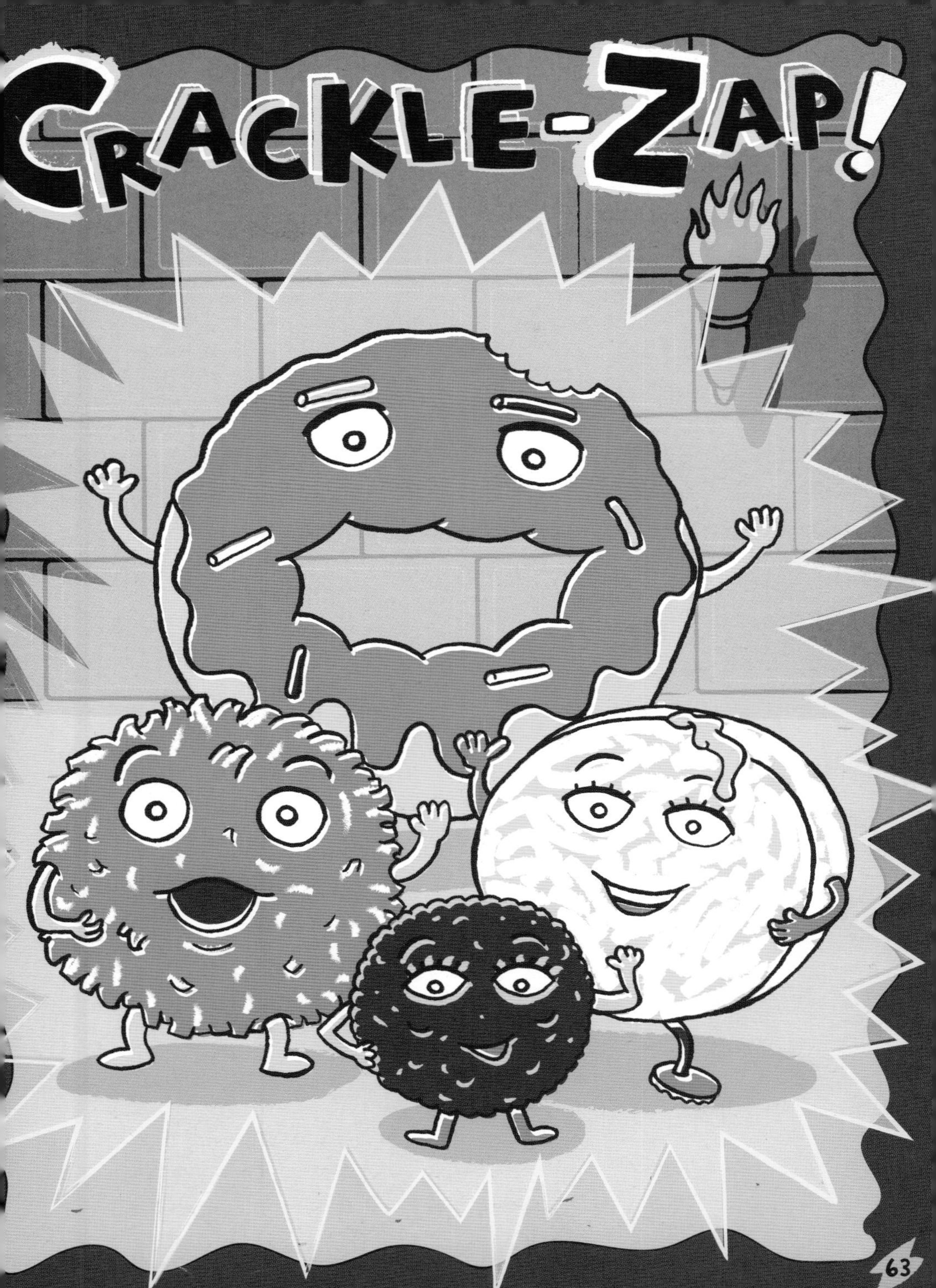
CRACKLE-ZAP!

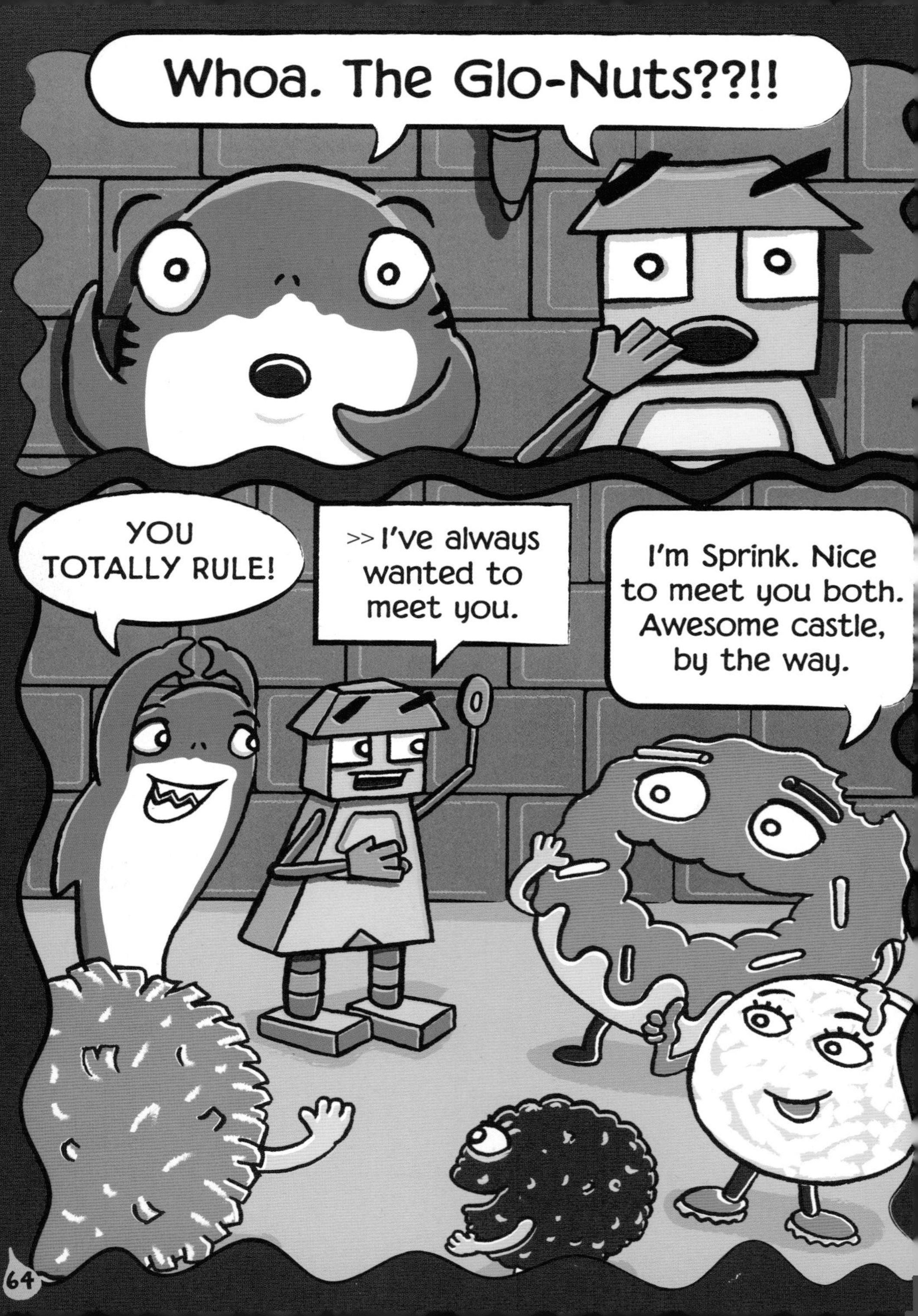

Whoa. The Glo-Nuts??!!
YOU TOTALLY RULE!
>> I've always wanted to meet you.
I'm Sprink. Nice to meet you both. Awesome castle, by the way.

Chapter 9

Bring String

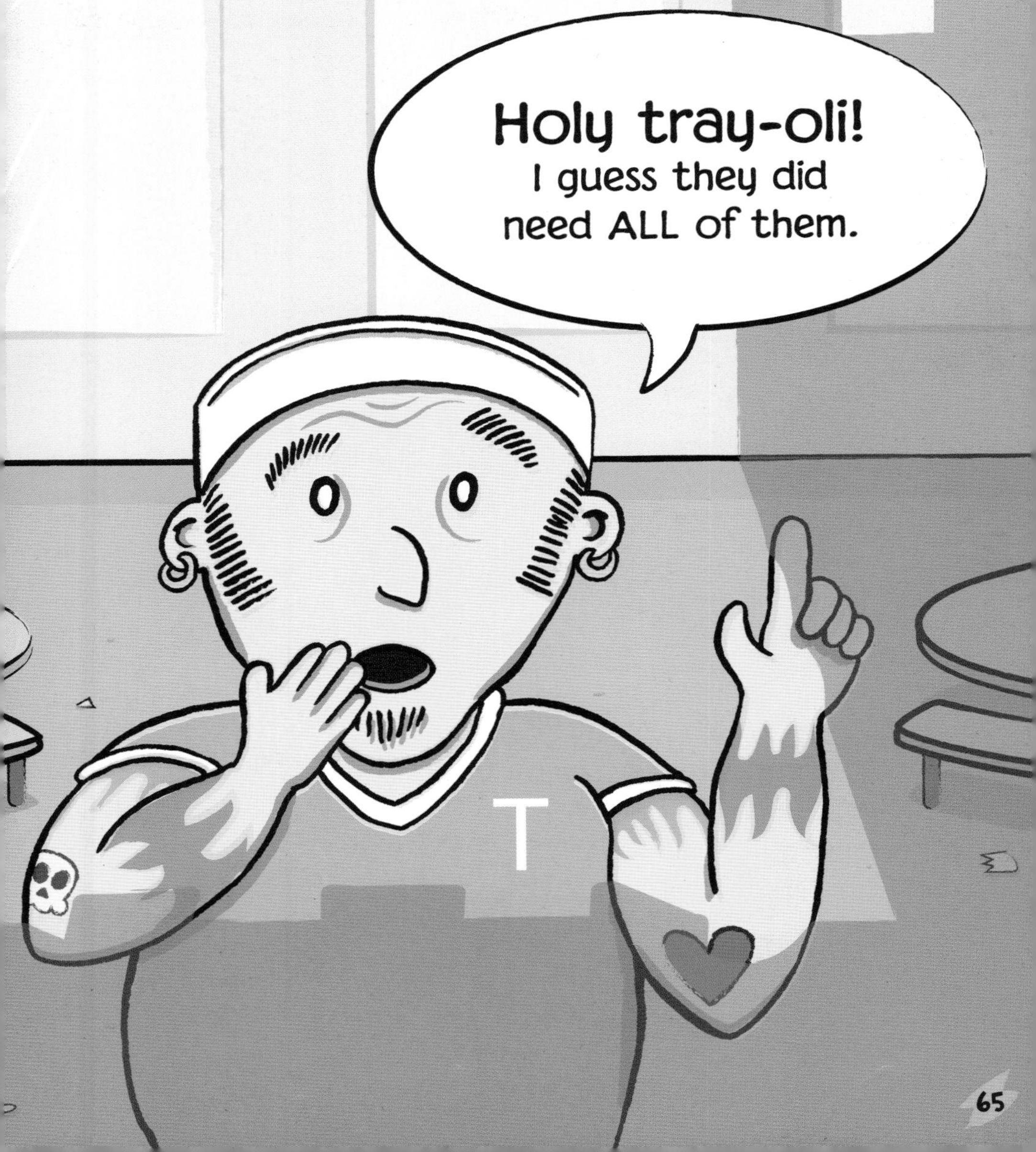
Holy tray-oli! I guess they did need ALL of them.

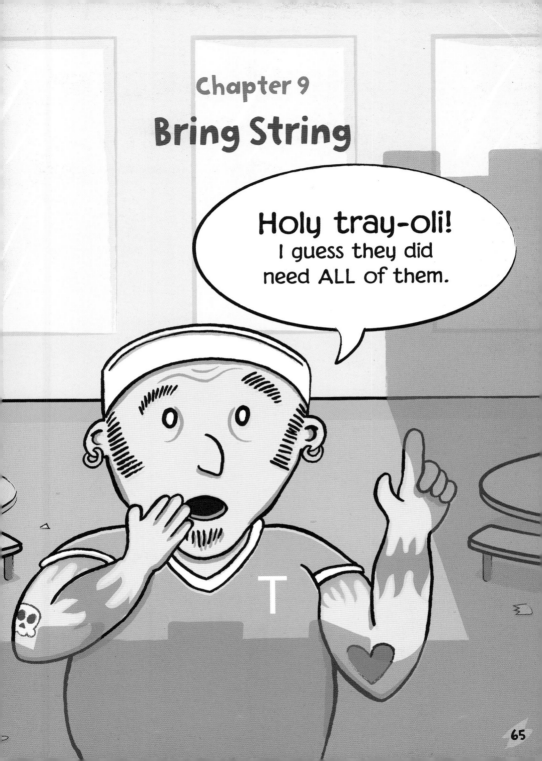

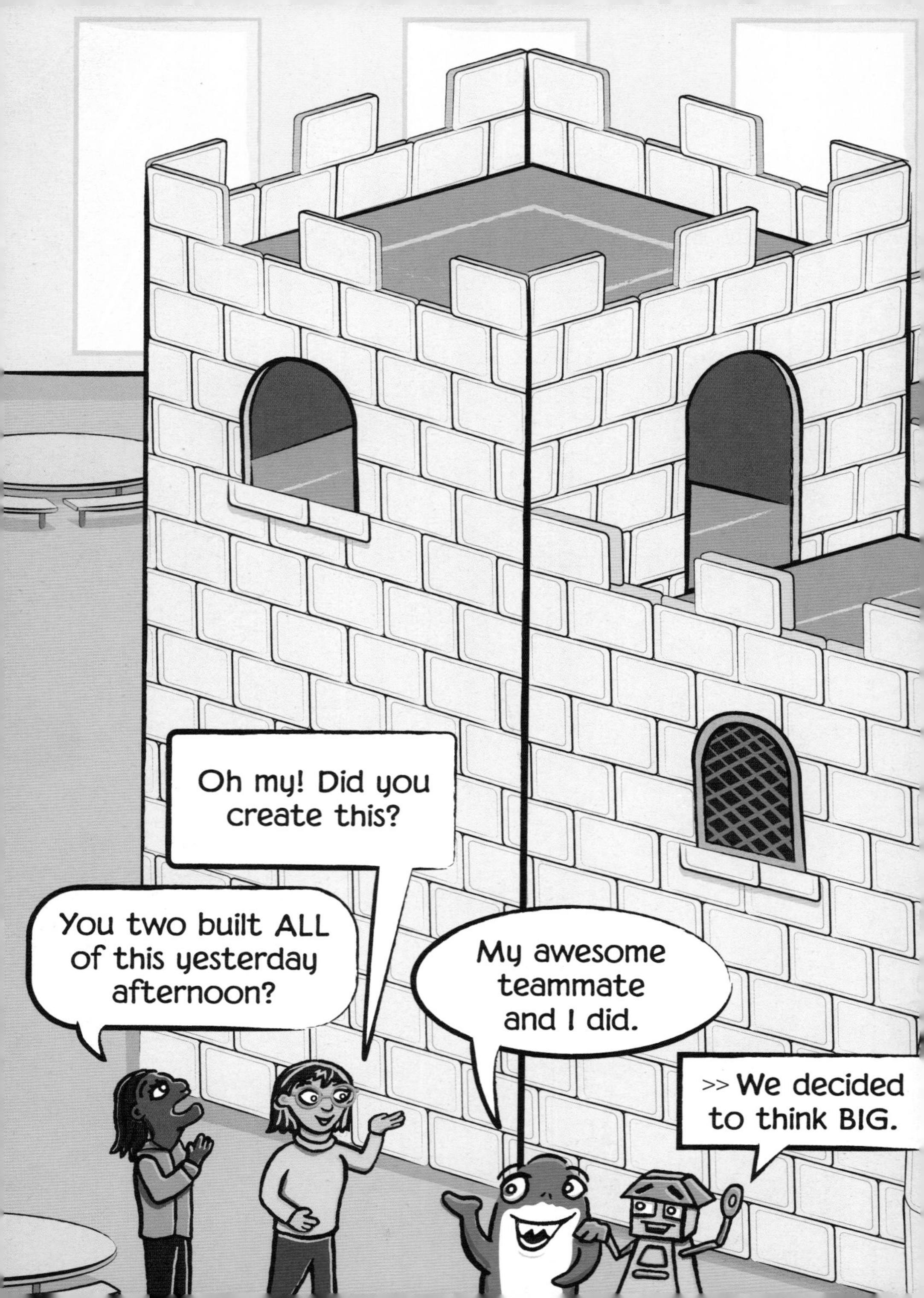
Oh my! Did you create this?
You two built ALL of this yesterday afternoon?
My awesome teammate and I did.
>> We decided to think BIG.

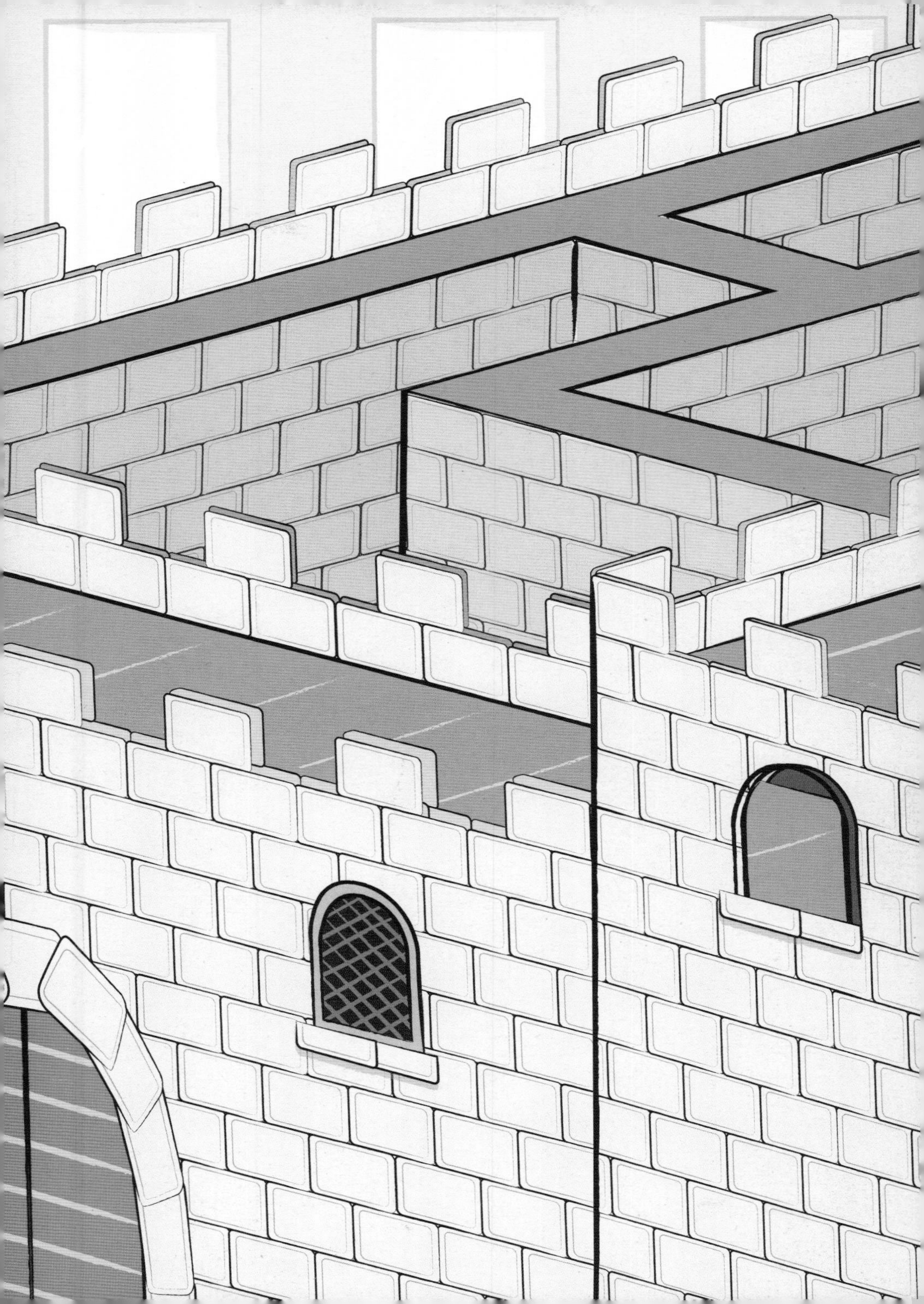

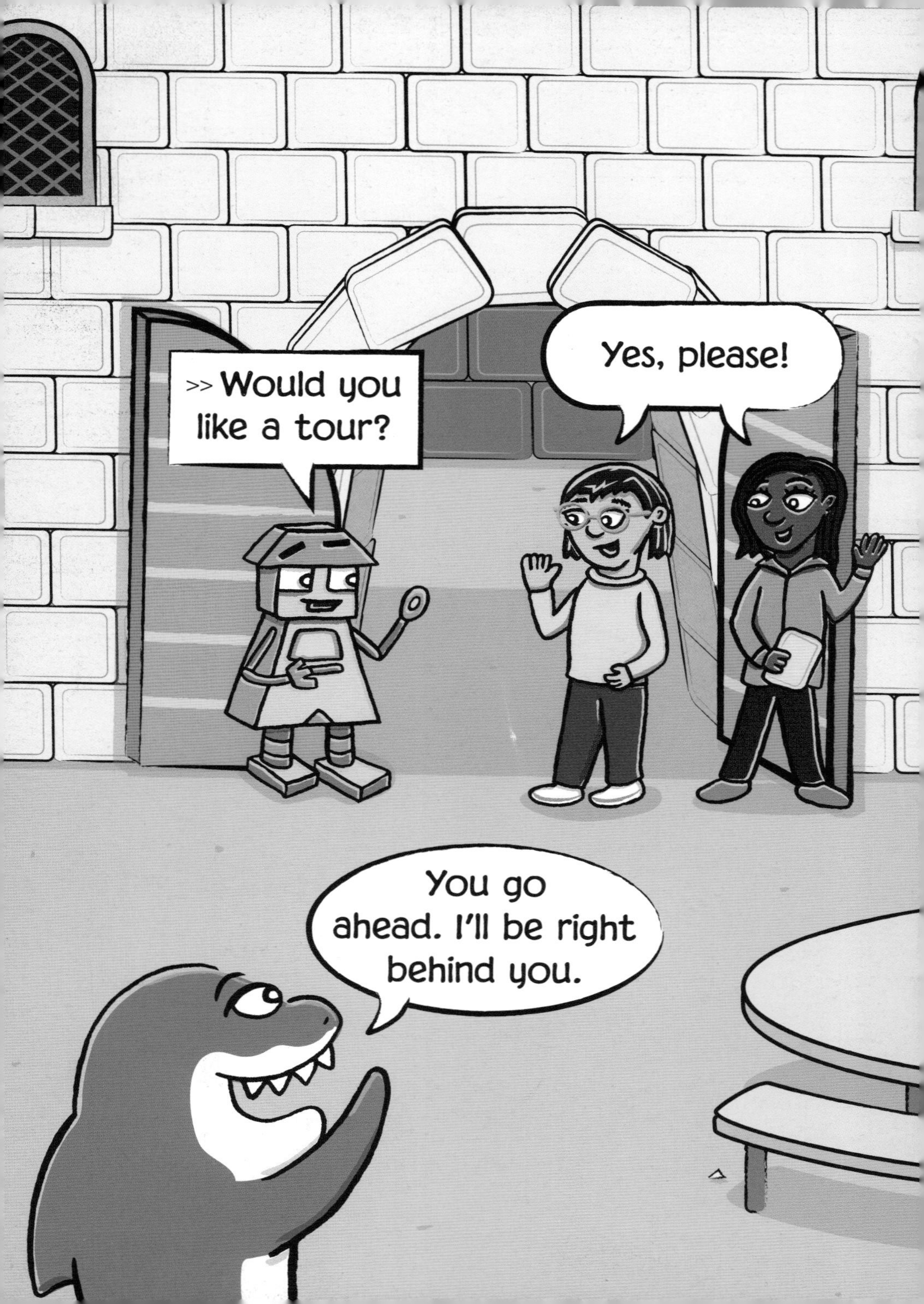
>> Would you like a tour?
Yes, please!
You go ahead. I'll be right behind you.

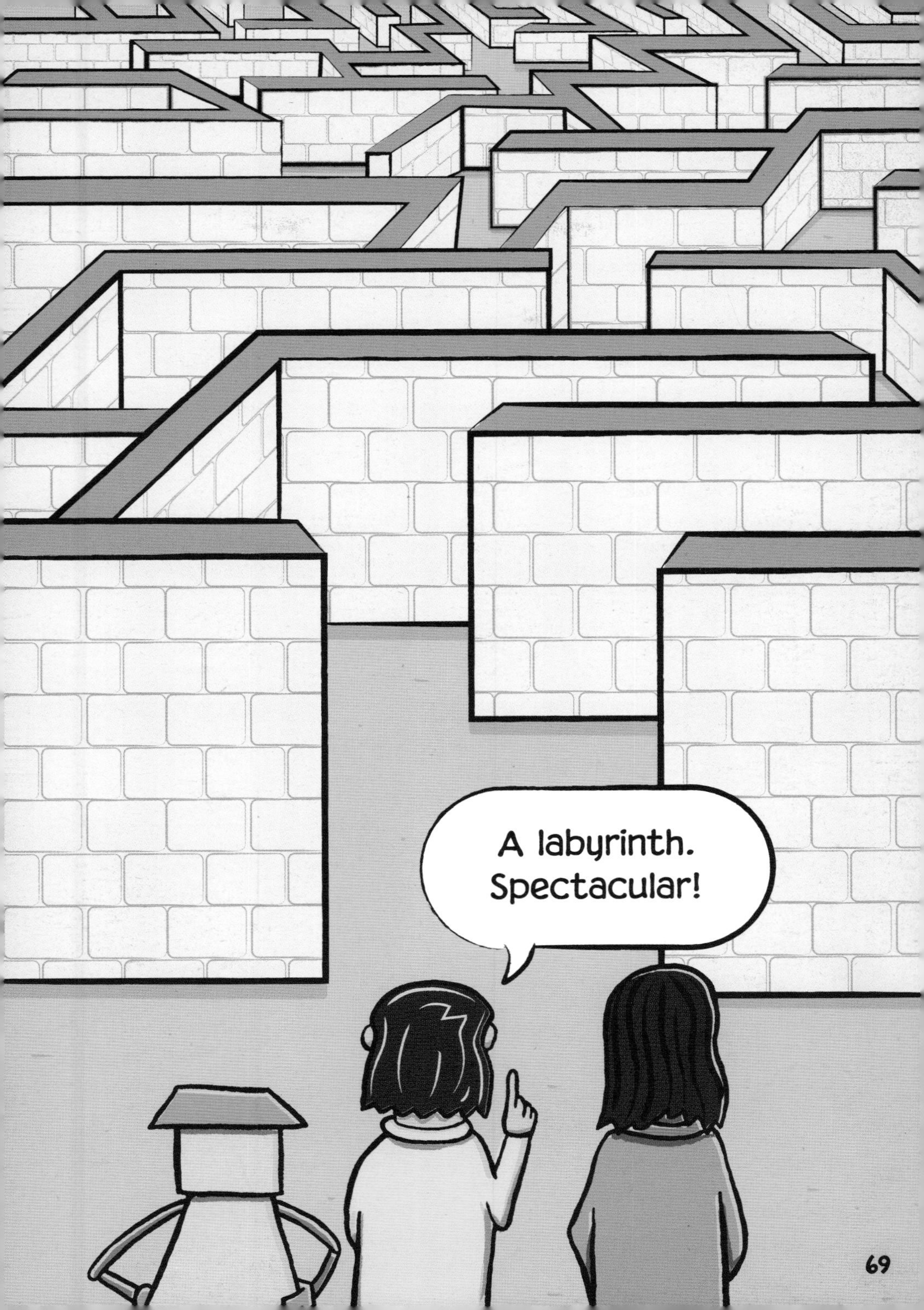
A labyrinth. Spectacular!

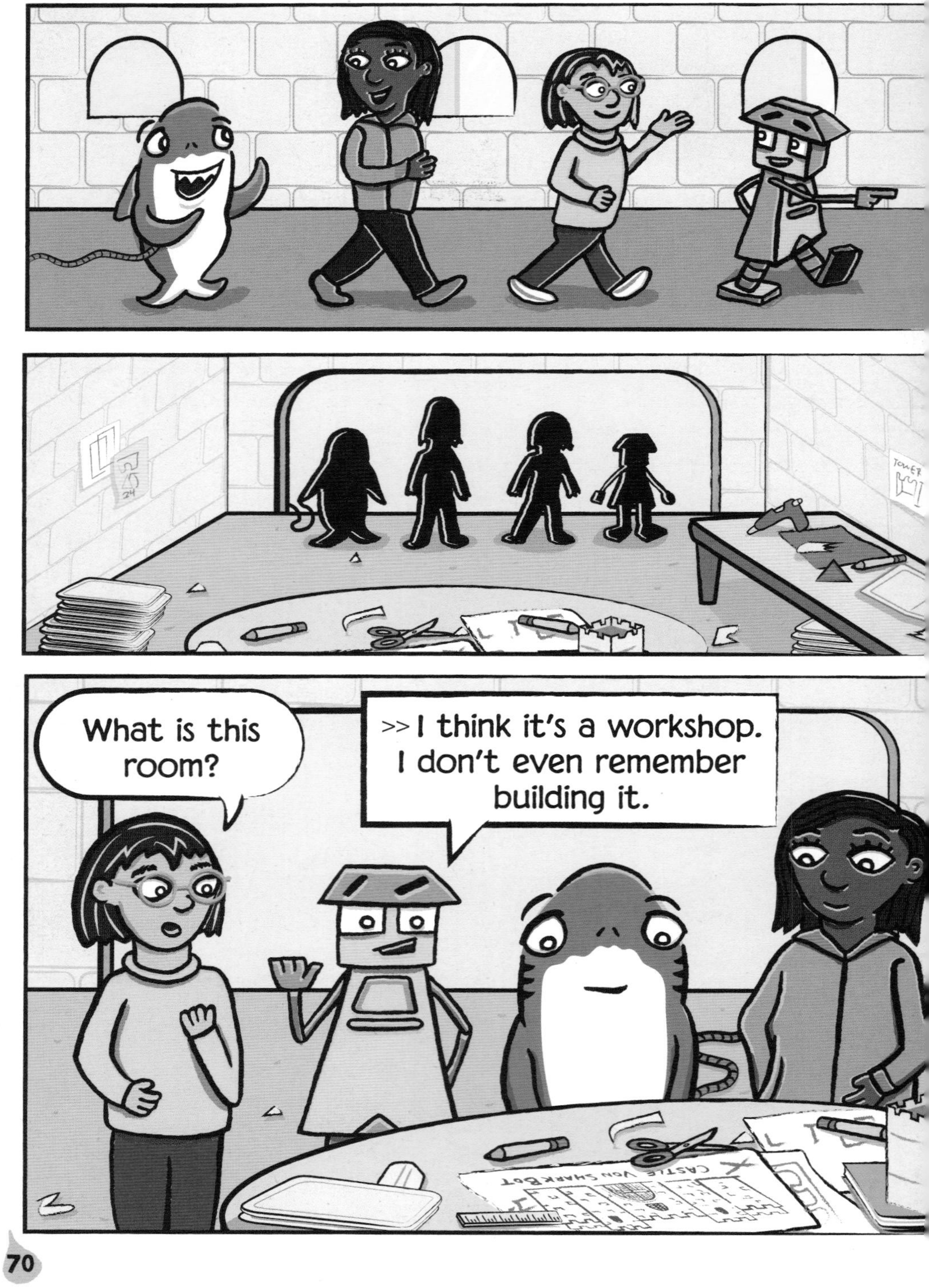
What is this room?
>> I think it's a workshop. I don't even remember building it.

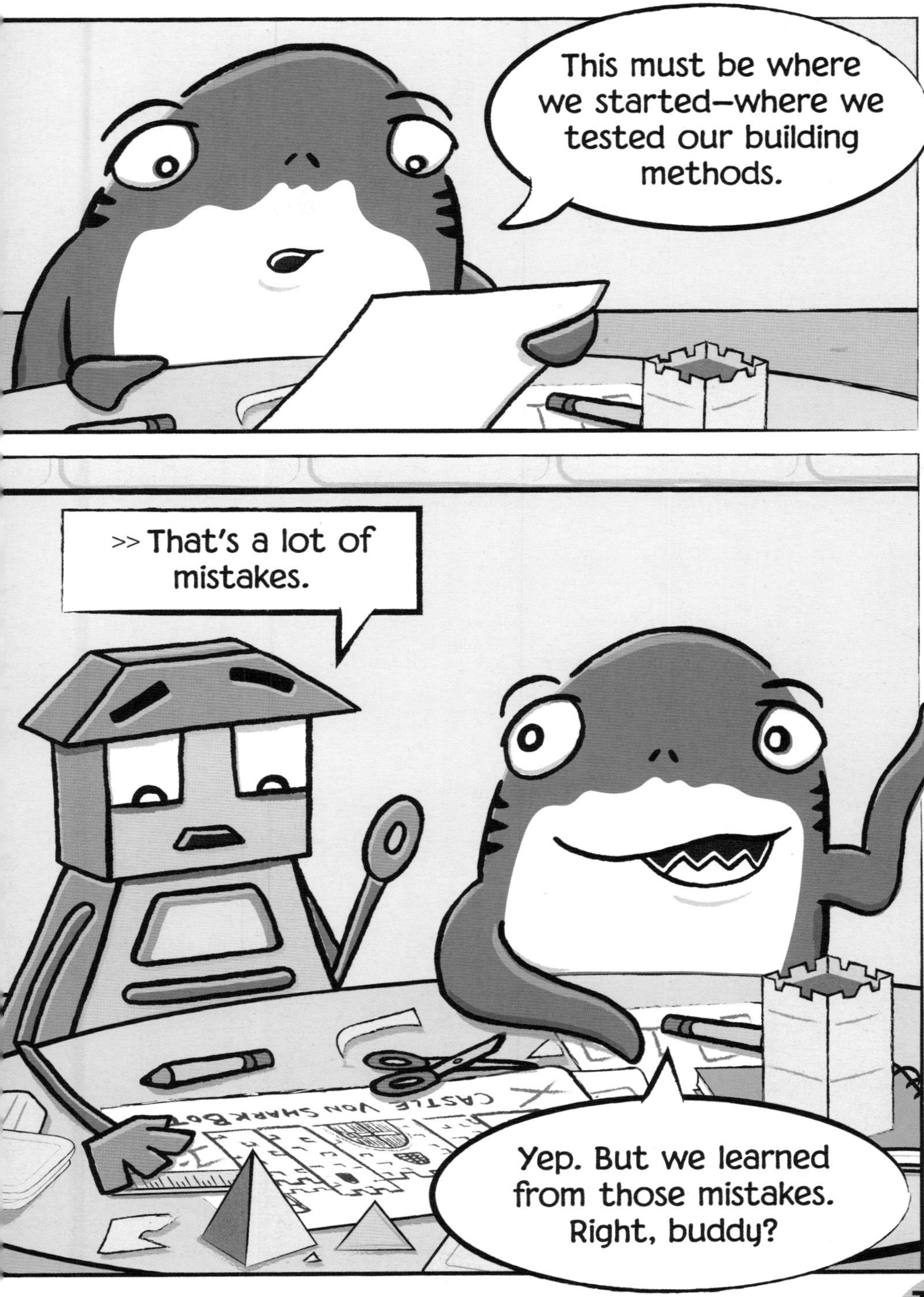
This must be where we started—where we tested our building methods.
>> That's a lot of mistakes.
CASTLE VON SHARKBOT
Yep. But we learned from those mistakes. Right, buddy?

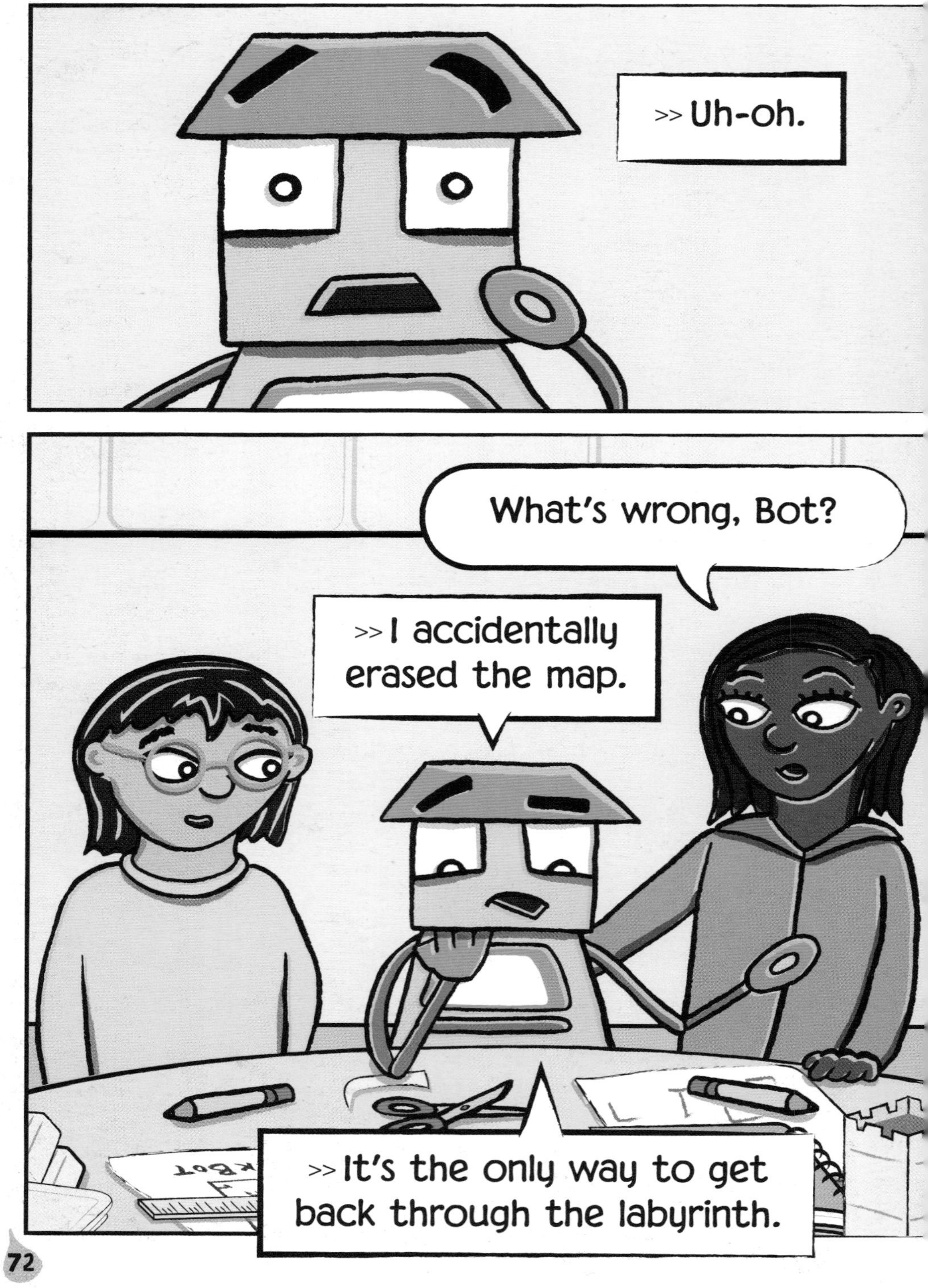
>> Uh-oh.
What's wrong, Bot?
>> I accidentally erased the map.
>> It's the only way to get back through the labyrinth.

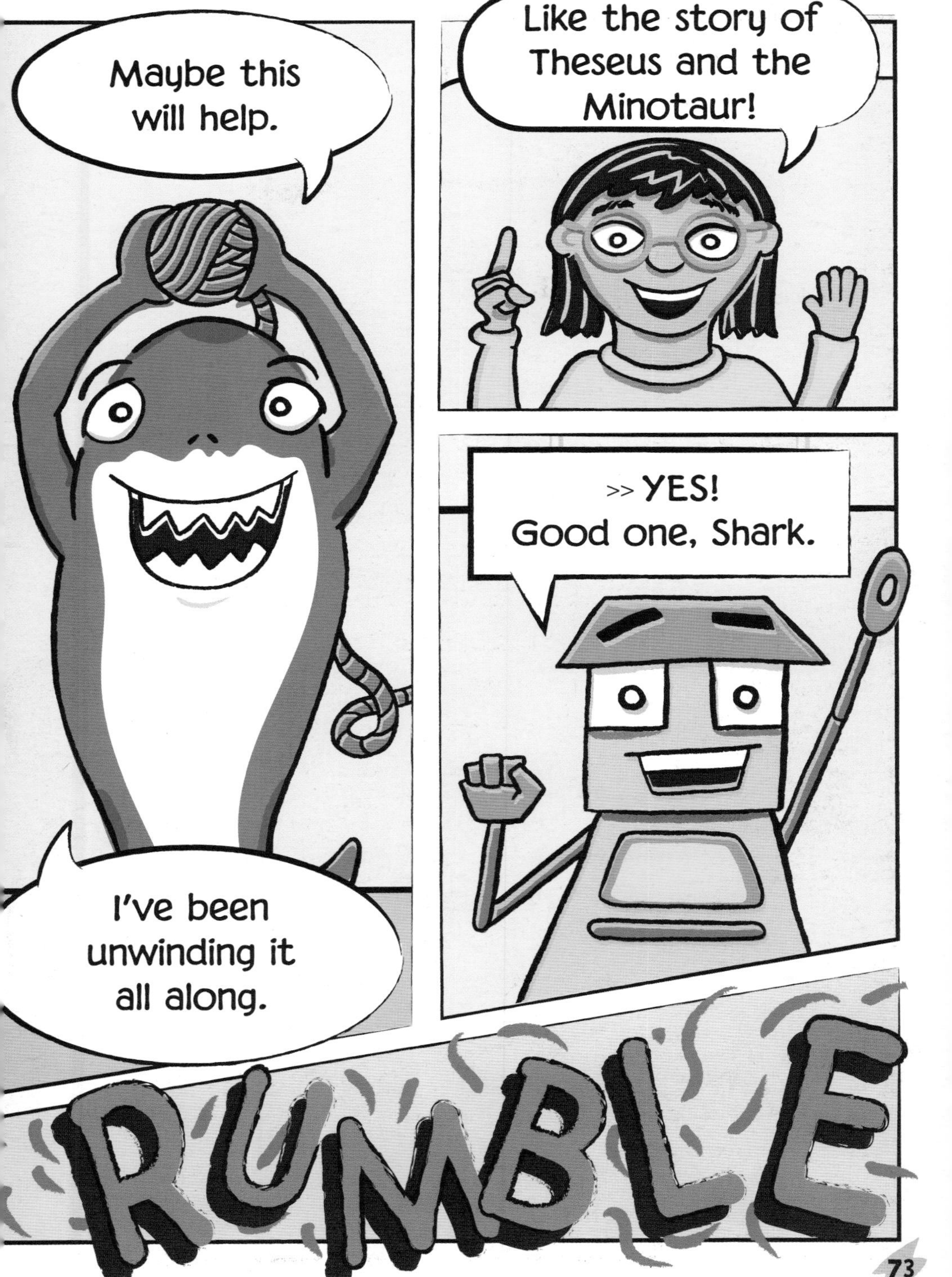
Maybe this will help.
Like the story of Theseus and the Minotaur!
>> YES! Good one, Shark.
I've been unwinding it all along.
RUMBLE

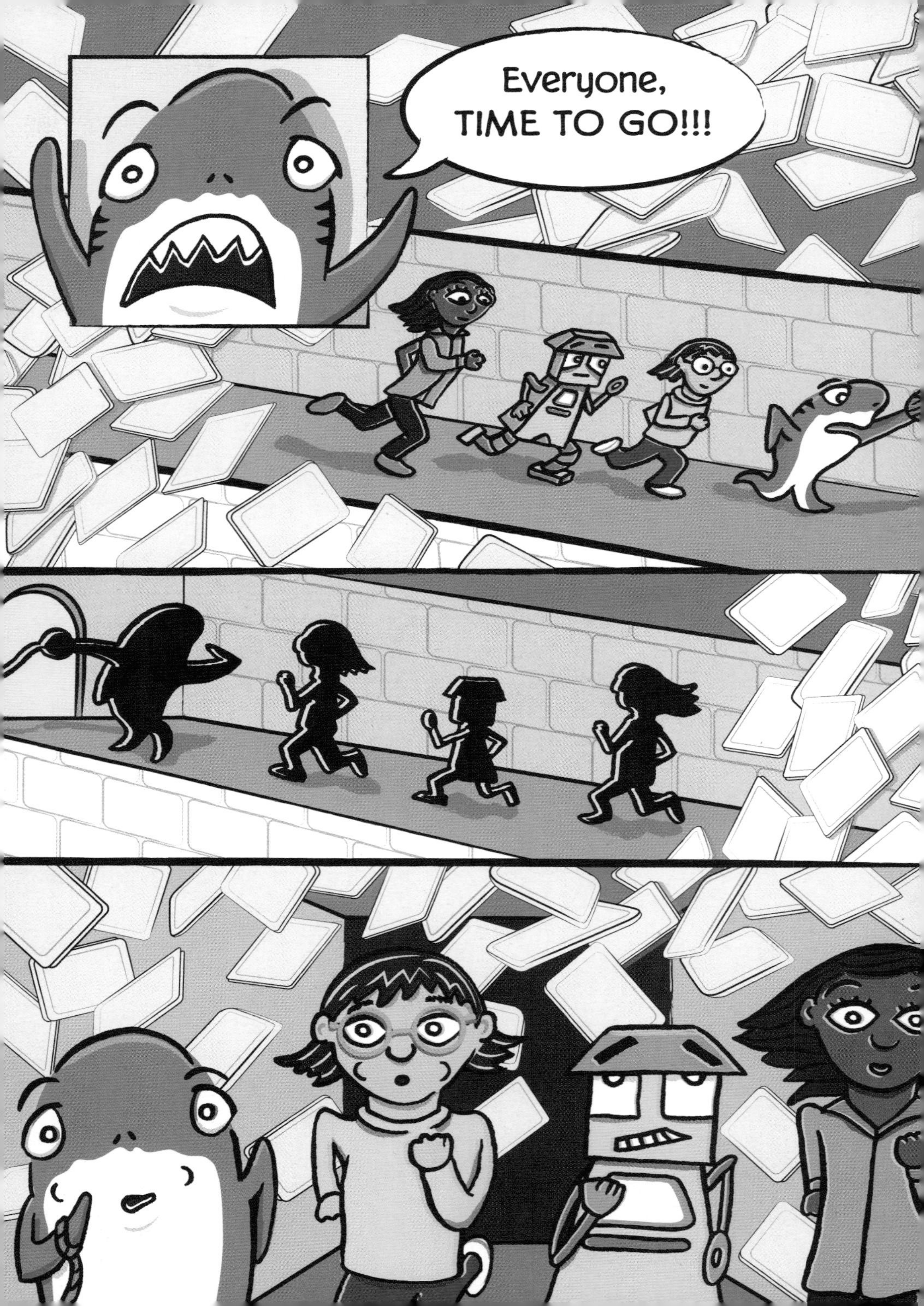
Everyone, TIME TO GO!!!

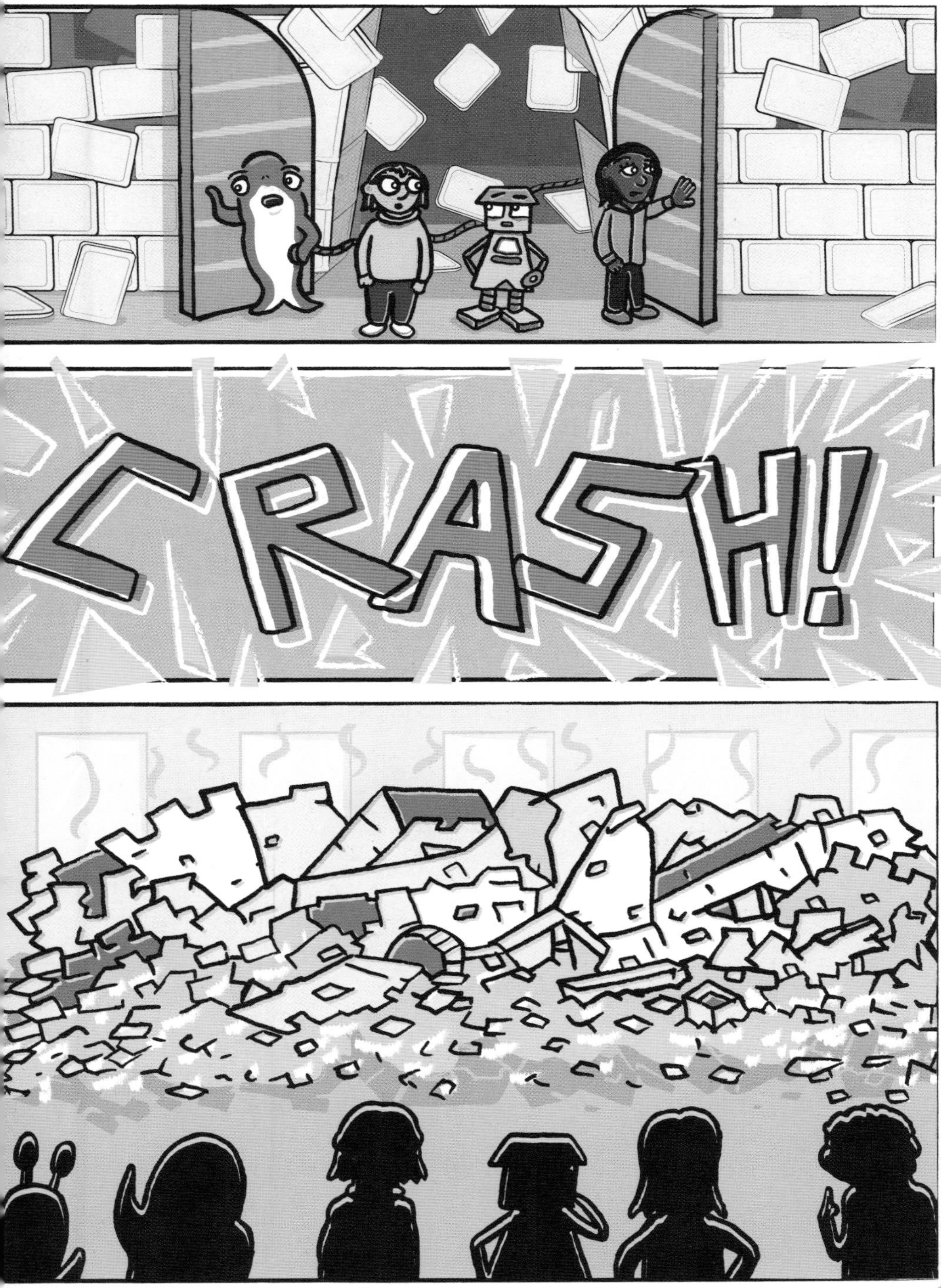
CRASH!

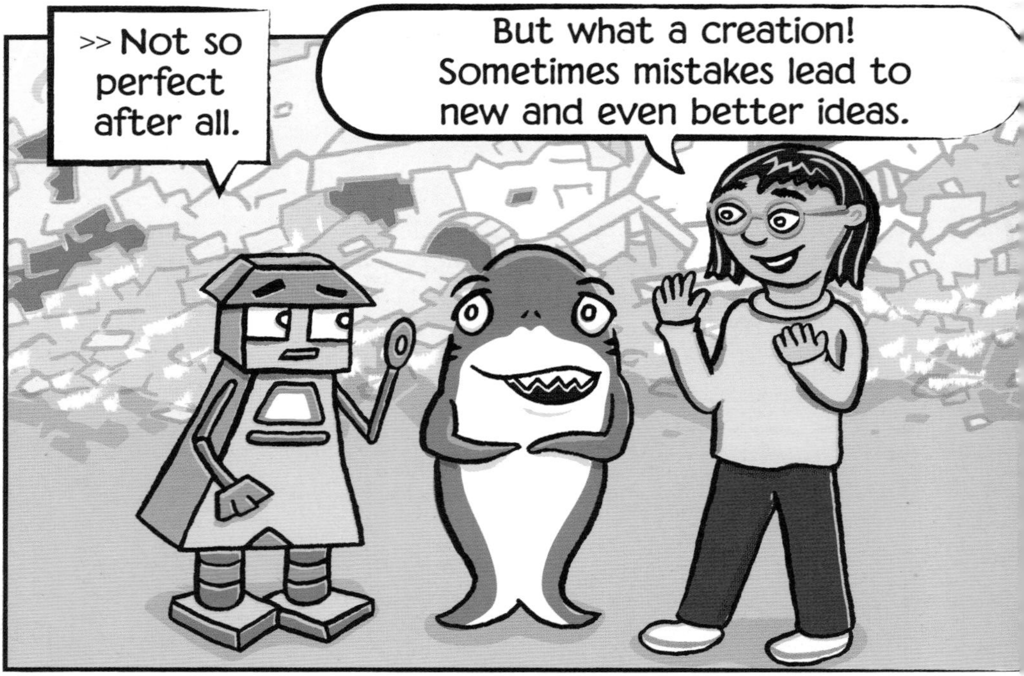
>> Not so perfect after all.
But what a creation! Sometimes mistakes lead to new and even better ideas.

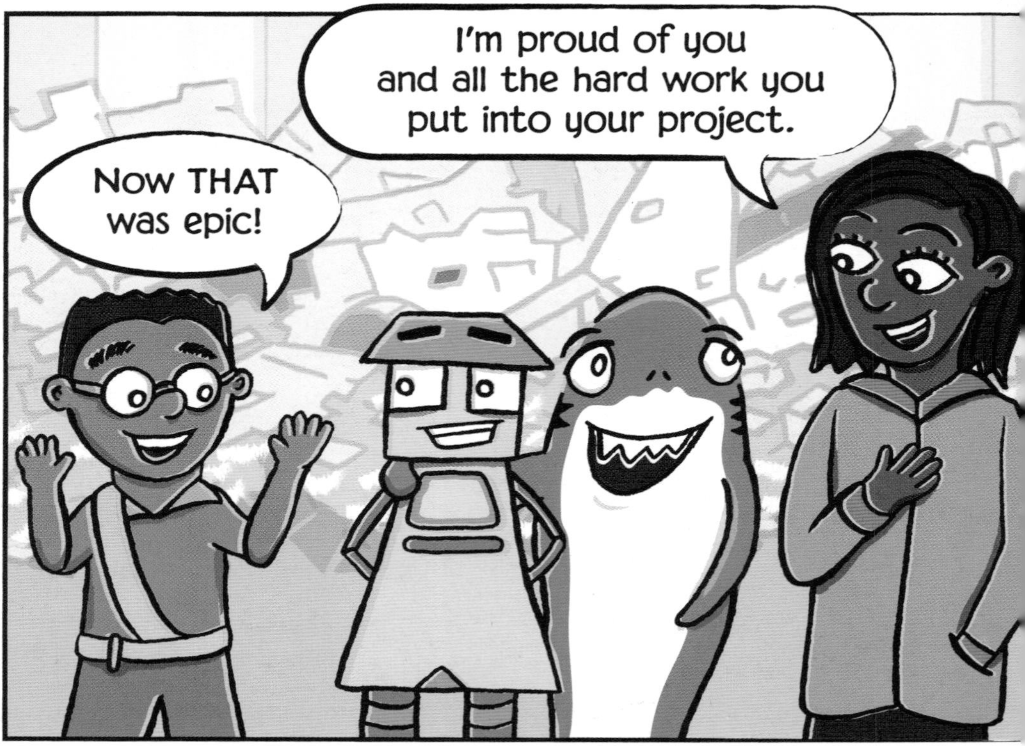
I'm proud of you and all the hard work you put into your project.
Now THAT was epic!

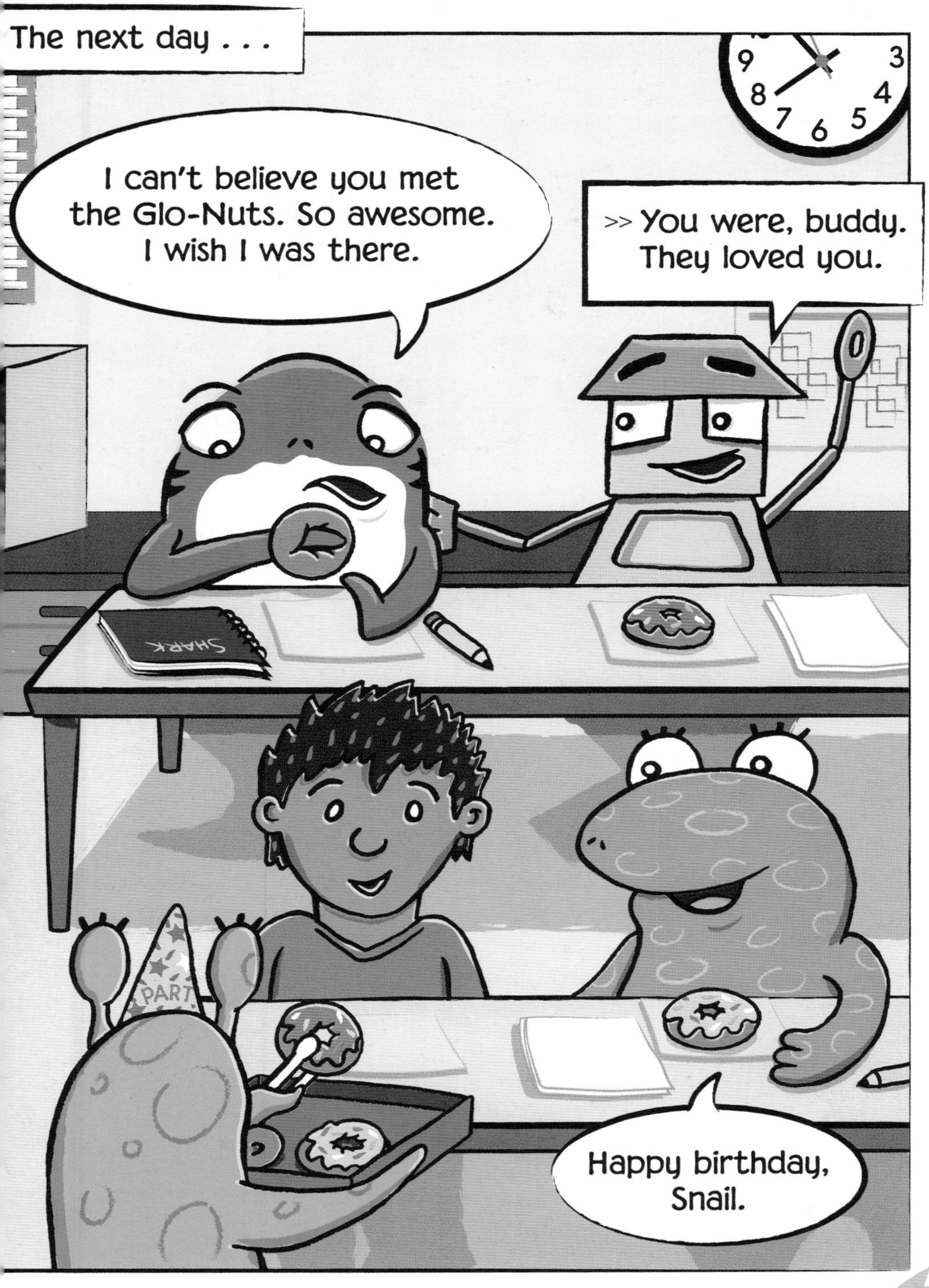

The next day . . .
I can't believe you met the Glo-Nuts. So awesome. I wish I was there.
>> You were, buddy. They loved you.
SHARK
PARTY
Happy birthday, Snail.

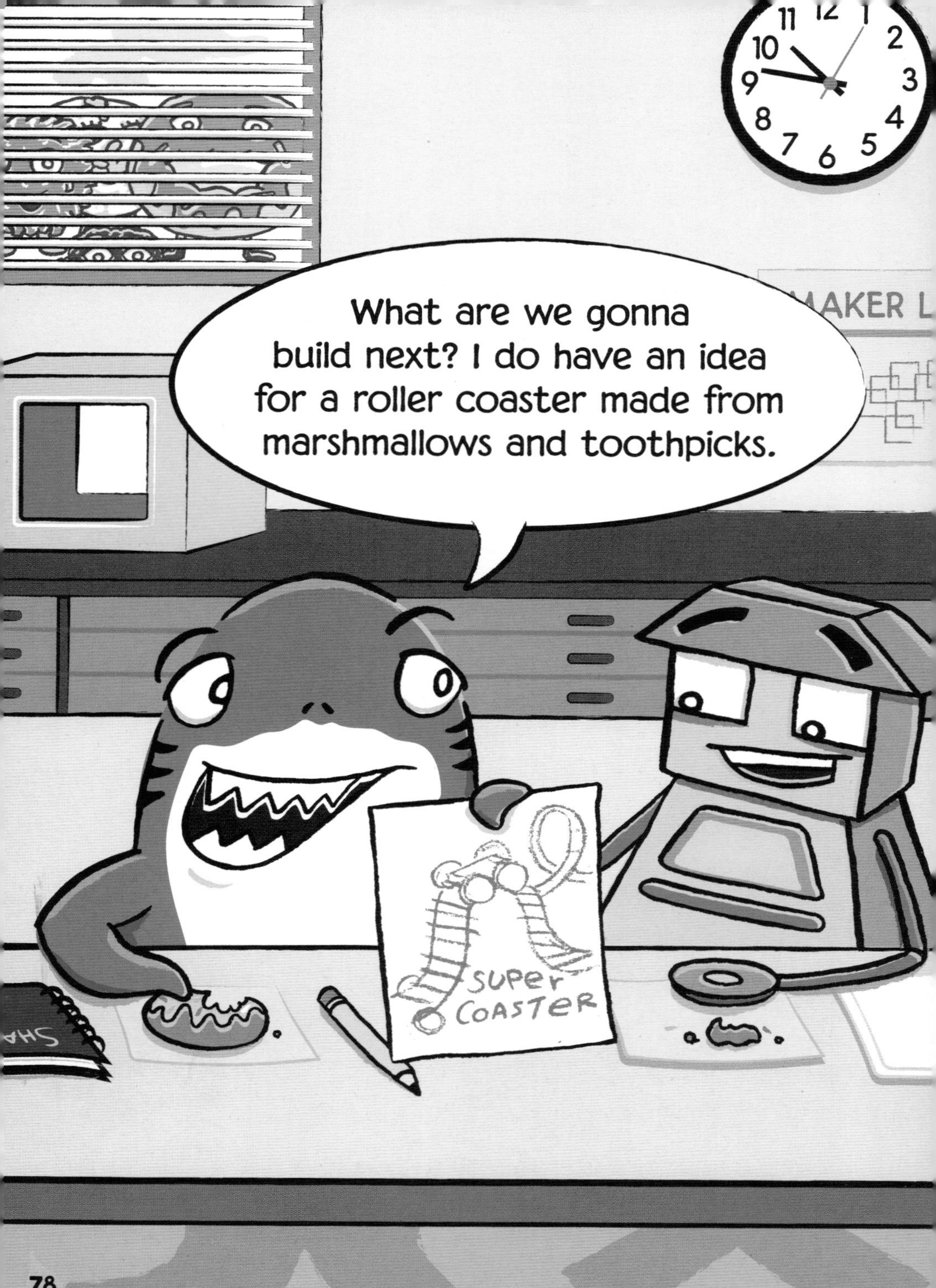

What are we gonna build next? I do have an idea for a roller coaster made from marshmallows and toothpicks.
SUPER COASTER

THE PAGE OF THANKS

by ~~Brain~~ *Brian* (with help from Bot)

1. These people made this book possible.

2. These people are cool. (So are my readers.)

Special thanks to Paul and Stephen Smith of
Yogasmiths UK; Tami Holihan-Frocchi;
my awesome editor Michelle Nagler — who always
makes my stories better; designer Jan Gerardi —
who puts these books together beautifully;
Jasmine Hodge for all her support at PRH;
my tireless agent Jennifer Unter; and my family,
who know that I am both part Shark and part Bot
and seem to be okay with that.

We've all been through a lot in the past couple
of years. Anxiety is a real thing, no matter
how old you are. It's nothing to be ashamed of,
and it's okay to ask for help when you need it.
(I felt anxious at times working on this book.)
Take a few breaths and know you won't feel that
way forever.

Be kind to each other.

* *

TAKE A BREATH
with Shark

Everyone has lots of different feelings EVERY day. Taking DEEP BREATHS can help you relax and face problems. **Give it a try!**

1 Sit in a comfortable spot and take a few quick breaths. Watch your belly go in and out.

2 Close your eyes.
Take a LONG, slow breath **IN** through your nose.
You can say "FIN - 2 - 3 - 4" in your head as you breathe in.

FIN - 2 - 3 - 4

3 Slowly say "SWIM BACK TO THE OCEAN SHORE" in your head as you breathe OUT through your mouth.

4 Repeat 3 times.

SWIM BACK TO THE OCEAN SHORE

Be like the water.

HOW TO DRAW A ZO-NUT

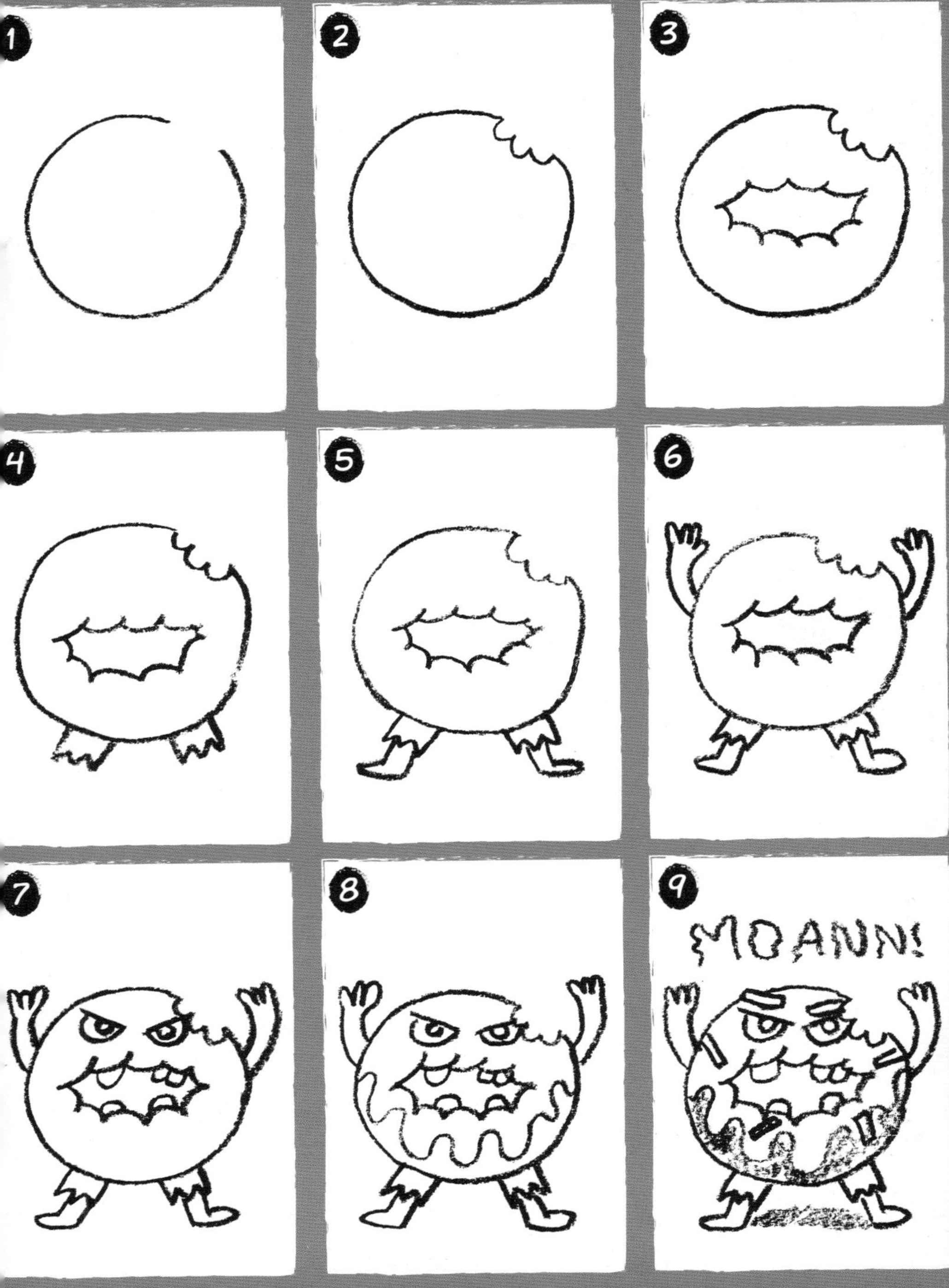
1
2
3
4
5
6
7
8
9
MOANN!

Brian Yanish has worked for Jim Henson Productions, trained as a special effects mold maker, written and performed comedy, and designed educational software, apparel, furniture, and toys. He is the creator of ScrapKins®, a recycled arts program that inspires kids to see creative potential in everyday junk. Brian has presented workshops at schools around the world and even appeared on *Sesame Street.* He lives in Rochester, New York, and enjoys sharks, robots, and gummy things.

brianyanish.com